Secrets and Vows

Secrets and Vows

W.C. Child

Red Pen Enterprises, LLC

Red Pen Enterprises, LLC

Copyright ©2020 by W. C. Child

ISBN: 97817322609-3-1
ePub ISBN: 97817322609-5-5
MOBI ISBN: 97817322609-4-8

Cover Design by Scott McWilliams Image by Muratart/Shutterstock.com
Printed in the United States of America.

Library of Congress Control Number: 2020942357

Red Pen Enterprises, LLC Clarksville, TN 37043

www.wcchildbooks.com

CHAPTER ONE

Identity Crisis

"This is WRPE coming to you with a live report. Police recently responded to the scene of a brutal attack of a pregnant woman in a suburban neighborhood just west of downtown. When paramedics arrived, the badly beaten woman was alive but in critical condition as she was rushed to the local medical center. According to our sources, police were sent to this address by a concerned relative. We will continue with updates as more details become available."

"How awful," I said to myself. "I hope they find the person responsible for the attack." My mind shifted from that tragedy to the anticipation of our anniversary celebration. The aroma of the dinner prepared by the private chef added a savory ambiance to the house as I put finishing touches on my hair and make-up.

We'd just sat down to enjoy our anniversary meal when the ring of the doorbell was followed by a loud knock. Curiosity led the way to the front door after we removed the napkins from our laps and abandoned our place settings. As we got closer to the front door, the white porch light mixed with the red and blue flashing lights of a police car and formed a blinking color wheel reminiscent of the American flag. I couldn't imagine why two police officers were at our home. When Carter stepped onto the porch, my foot prevented the door from closing before I could get outside. I rubbed away the chill from the October breeze but couldn't shake the fear in the pit of my stomach.

The officers presented an authoritative aura, quite the opposite from the Barney Fife character I often laughed about on television. Their dark blue uniforms were accented by silver badges, colorful patches, handcuffs, communication equipment, and a gun. While one officer spoke, the other kept his thumb hooked in his belt close to his gun. In his friendliest voice, one officer said, "Good evening, sir. Ma'am."

Carter looked over his left shoulder and gave me a disapproving look before he said, "Good evening, officers. How can I help you?"

"We have an arrest warrant for Ben Wilson. Sir, are you, Mr. Wilson?"

"No, I'm not," he responded with a surprised look on his face. "My name is Carter Mann."

"Does Ben Wilson live here?"

"Sir, no one by that name lives here. Are you sure you have the correct address?"

"Pretty sure. We're at the address on the arrest warrant."

"Then I don't know what to tell you. I'm not Ben Wilson."

The officer paused, then said, "How long have you lived here, sir?"

"Since the house was built. We're the only ones who've ever lived here."

After looking down at the warrant, then up at Carter, he said, "Give me a minute, sir. I'm sure we can clear this up shortly." After a hushed conversation between themselves, he walked down the steps to the squad car while his partner remained on the porch.

While we waited for him to return, I said to Carter, "Do you know who he's talking about? Who is Ben Wilson?"

Carter glanced at the officer standing four feet away from us and said, "Like I told them, I don't know Ben Wilson. Obviously, this is a case of mistaken identity, or they're at the wrong address. Let me handle this, Grace. Go back inside."

I heard him but didn't move. Newly found bravery surged without considering the repercussions I'd probably face later. I didn't care. Shaving the truth was Carter's specialty. I wanted to hear the real-time conversation, not the redacted version I'd get from him. Remaining on the porch was worth the risk. Before Carter could repeat his demand, a scratchy voice from the walkie-talkie said, "Tell Mr. Mann we need to see some identification."

I stayed on the porch while Carter retrieved his driver's license. Because his car and physical description on his license matched the suspect's, the questions continued. Carter's vehement denial of brutally assaulting a pregnant woman and having an alias sounded convincing until he said, "I would never assault a woman." I immediately looked down; I was afraid my eyes would verify they'd found the right person. Less than an hour ago, the radio broadcast reported a horrible story about an assault. The similarities between the questions from the police and the news story sounded too familiar to be coincidental. But how could that be? He's been with either the kids or me all day. I finished those thoughts in time to hear Carter's offer to appear at the police station with his attorney the next day being drowned out by the reading of the Maranda warning. His look of confidence morphed into repugnance after the handcuffs opened their mouth wider than Pac Man and gobbled up his freedom. After a polite salutation directed at me, the officers escorted my impeccably dressed husband down the steps and away from our anniversary celebration. With hands behind his back and wrists adorned with silver restraints,

Carter and his spotless public image were placed in the back of the police car.

Like fireworks on the 4th of July, shock and disbelief exploded multiple times in my head. A million thoughts flooded my mind as my eyes followed the slow-moving, one-car parade down the driveway. There was nothing I could do but watch my husband be driven away in glorified fashion. The Independence Day symbolism starkly contrasted with Carter's arrest. To his horror, all the neighbors were watching. For years, I'd been punished for the possibility of ruining his reputation. How ironic he'd manifested his public demise in less than ten minutes. At the end of the driveway, the police car's red and blue lights stopped flashing. The light on the porch returned to white, and the viewing slits in the curtains of the adjacent houses closed. The show was over.

CHAPTER TWO

The Morning After

Where am I, was my first thought the minute my left eye opened and tried to focus on my surroundings. Nothing felt normal because nothing was. The compressed sightlines only allowed slivers of brightness to filter through my eyelashes. The pins of light were harsh and caused shadows to form around objects in the room. I blinked quickly, hoping to improve my vision. My left eye remained lazy and only did half its job. It wanted no part of the full spectrum of the piercing light. I tried to open my right eye to view more of the room. That was more than enough to make me want to shut off all external contact with the world and close both eyes again. I needed time for the grogginess to subside and the drum solo in my head to quiet down so my mind could catch up. I placed my arm back over my eyes to block the light. Too late. It already saw me.

I continued to lay there, hoping motivation would become my ally, but it didn't. My focus turned to the steady sound of bells. It was too bright for the clock to chime only five times. If that clock was right, inside my house, daylight and darkness never traded places. Instead of being in my favorite pajamas, snuggled underneath the fluffy down comforter, I was curled up on the sofa under a throw blanket,

5

and every light in the house was on. Instead of the plump goose down pillows, my head rested on stiff substitutes, half their size and without the familiar lavender smell. Since I'd fallen asleep in my makeup, my eyeliner and mascara were smeared, my eyelash extensions compromised and only lipstick that wasn't transferred to the rim of the whiskey glass remained.

A sharp pain radiated up the back of my neck when I tried to reposition my body. The grimace on my face justified the expletive my tongue couldn't control once the throbbing pain intensified in my head. Any further movements would be deliberate and spaced apart. I took my time sitting up, before putting both feet on the floor and trying to stand. The weight of the prior evening and the burgeoning hangover from the massive amounts of alcohol I drank, held me in place as I rested my head in my hands. Though the special reserve temporarily numbed my pain, it couldn't wipe out everything I wanted to forget. For years, I'd feared an angry husband or boyfriend, intent on defending the honor of his family or significant other with either a fist or a gun, would show up at our door, looking for my husband. Carter would absorb the threats, deny the allegations, and each man would walk away with pieces of their dignity intact. I never imagined a police officer with an arrest warrant would be the man with a gun on the other side of the door. Thank God our children weren't home.

I forced myself to stand and shuffle toward the kitchen. Coffee was what I needed most. I lost my appetite after the police arrested Carter and tried to drink away my sorrows. Now I needed a different drink to clear my mind. The aroma of the brew wafted up to my nose in anticipation of the first luxurious sip of coffee. The hot liquid cut a path across my tongue and down my throat, pulling with it the stale taste of any residual alcohol. When the first swallow reached the bottom of my empty stomach, I was surprised steam didn't come from my nostrils. Several sips later, mental clarity started to nudge me back to reality as my mind continued to awaken and roam into places filled with regret and disappointment.

I looked at my garments and began to think about the plans I'd made for our celebration. No matter how he treated me all the other days of the year, Carter always made me feel special on our anniversary. On that day, I could forget about all the other dysfunction in our marriage and imagine we were truly committed to each other. And for the fifteen days, we were. No kids, no work, no external distractions. Just us two. I'd focus on making myself radiantly beautiful for my husband and plan the meal. He'd take the children to my parents, arrange surprise deliveries, and present me with a special gift during dinner. The next day we'd sleep late, enjoy each other again, and catch an afternoon flight to a tropical destination.

When I heard our daughter speaking to him on the phone, I knew there'd been a change in plans. The frustration came through his voice about the delay and his preference to be at home. Between demanding clients, extended meetings, and changed flights, he wouldn't be home until the morning of our anniversary. The genuineness expressed in his words tugged at my heart and demonstrated the value he placed on our anniversary celebration. When he walked through the door the following day with a smile on his face and a bouquet of my favorite flowers, it made me happy—— so happy that I missed the giant red flag.

CHAPTER THREE

Bullhorn

I passed by the dining room and looked at a table with an uneaten meal, unused place settings, and napkins thrown haphazardly between the tapered candles. Our anniversary dinner had been ruined. I began to clear the table in the same dress I'd been wearing the night before. My wrinkled garment reminded me of what could've been. My expectation for a celebration drove away in a red and blue light show that none of our neighbors would ever forget. Neither the exclusive designer nor I intended for this special garment to be worn while performing waitressing duties, but I was improvising. On my final trip to the sink, anger crept up my spine and through my fingers as the weight of the evening's sorrow piled onto the plates. The sink was the recipient of my ire. A jigsaw puzzle with missing pieces remained after disconnected slivers of glass took refuge on the floor. The good china was suddenly missing two pieces. I looked down at the broken plates and thought about my night of unfulfilled expectations. I began to cry and cried until there were no more tears. It was time to change out of my anniversary dinner clothes into something more appropriate for cleaning.

The eerie silence of our home overwhelmed me once the ringing sounds of the broken dishes and my sniffles subsided. I needed a distraction to help get me out of my funk. I turned on the radio and sighed with relief when voices chased away the loneliness. My peace was short-lived. The music was interrupted by distracting words.

"We interrupt this program to bring you late-breaking news. WRPE has just confirmed that prominent business-man Carter Mann was arrested last night under the alias, Ben Wilson, and charged with aggravated domestic assault and violence against a fetus. The victim, who hasn't been identi-fied, was not the spouse of the accused. Mr. Mann is scheduled for an arraignment and bond hearing on Monday. We will keep you updated as more details become available."

The music returned in the middle of the lyrics as if nothing had changed. I sat wide-eyed and frozen, still pro-cessing the news like everyone else who'd been listening to that station. Carter's arrest was no longer a secret from our friends, family, neighbors, children, and his business associ-ates. A lifetime of lies had publicly exploded in our faces. I could no longer protect his infidelity or our other marital secrets. We'd both been exposed. It would become evident that his actions against that woman were not a first for him. His ugly secret was no longer hidden from the world. It was front-page news.

I jumped at the sound of the phone and let it ring until it stopped. Fear kept me from answering. I didn't want to answer the rhetorical question, "What happened?" or any other false declaration of concern. In my head, I heard words from the people I was avoiding.

"Grace, I know you're there. Pick up, please." "Did you know about the affair?" "I feel so sorry for you, Grace. Is there anything I can do?" "How long has he been cheating on you?" "Let me know when you're ready to talk. I'm here for you." "Answer the phone, Grace. You can't hide for-ever." "Why did you stay with him?"

I wasn't ready to hear what anybody else thought about me, my husband, or our marriage. It was none of their busi-ness. The weight of those conversations, real and contrived, sat on my heart. I screamed from my soul until I drowned out the radio announcer's voice, the music, and the phone before I keeled over into a heap on the sofa, in the dress from my anniversary date, and sobbed.

As much as I wanted to remain cradled in defeat and sorrow, I knew it wouldn't accomplish anything. I had to face the reality of public exposure and prepare for the aftermath. A long, hot shower and a change of clothes was where I would start. The constant flow of warm water loosened up my stiff neck as the aroma of the body wash relaxed my mind. The soothing sounds of the water lulled me into the memories of last night and beyond. I suddenly felt attacked and being forced to deal with the truth of my existence with my husband. I couldn't ignore the amplified psychological and physical trauma that constantly surrounded our marriage. Despite my longing for a true marriage filled with love and honesty, it never fully materialized. Over the years, I'd been able to block out what I wanted and view our marriage through my tolerance filters. Although far from ideal, I became accustomed to his ways and made adjustments to keep him happy. What he did and didn't do was kept between us. I protected our status as much as he did. Our reasons were different, but we shared a common goal to protect our image at all costs. But after last night, more secrets than I knew about were revealed in the most visually dramatic way possible. Pandora's box had opened, and I didn't want to think about what was coming out next.

Chapter Four

Cupid's Arrow

Without a doubt, one of those unanswered phone calls was from my mother. I knew I needed to check on the kids, but couldn't bring myself to call her. Maybe tomorrow. For now, they'd be better off with my parents than with me for the next two weeks. I needed time to fall apart and wallow in self-pity and humiliation. I didn't want to talk to anyone yet. No one would understand. Imagining the disappointed faces of my family and friends caused me to pour a glass of wine. It didn't matter that it was barely 10:00 a.m. For the remainder of the day, I sat on the sofa, drinking, and thinking. I kept trying to find thoughts to replace the sights and sounds of the last twenty-four hours. Near the middle of the second bottle of wine, the shift occurred. Fond memories of our love story took center stage. Induced by nostalgia, or maybe inebriation, a familiar tingly feeling engulfed me when I thought about the first time I saw Carter. A chance encounter led to the beginning of our unforgettable love story. Those were the memories I wanted to focus on leading up to his first day in court, not the public spectacle the neighbors witnessed on our front porch.

I remembered how the sight of Carter sitting near the window inside my favorite coffee shop stopped me in my tracks. The jacket draped over the back of his chair, along with the crisp white shirt and designer tie, accented his well-groomed face and hair. The papers spread on the table

11

garnered his full attention as he raised the cup to and from his lips without looking up. Immediately, I looked at his ring finger. It was empty. I mentally celebrated that discovery and internally yelled "YES"! I didn't hear a word my friend said once he looked up from his papers and smiled at me. I was mesmerized by his eyes and beautiful smile. We felt an unbelievable attraction in a single fleeting glance. He was one of the best things I'd seen in a while. Had my friend not tugged on my arm, I believe I could have become an impromptu statue randomly placed in front of the coffee shop. But the end of the semester was near, and the statistics final needed my undivided attention. As she pulled me away, I prayed he would be there again when I had more time. My eyes hadn't seen enough yet.

Over the next two months, I frequently walked by the coffee shop hoping to catch another glimpse of the person responsible for the spike in my step count. Stalking was a bit strong to describe my persistence; following up seemed more appropriate. Some days I'd sit at his table by the window, drinking coffee I didn't want, waiting for someone I may never see again. On the day I was ready to abandon further expectations of meeting him, there he was, sitting alone at our table. I felt my heart beating double time as my mind and feet were at odds about what to do. As crazy as it felt, I didn't stop to admire the masculine window dressing I was convinced the coffee shop hired to lure women inside. I pretended he was the heavyset man with the beard filled with crumbs or the red-headed woman who always kept her glasses on top of her head. Neither were interesting enough to elevate my heart rate or cause me to stop. To pretend not to notice him was difficult, but strategic. I wanted to appear uninterested if he happened to glance my way. Although risky, I believe it added intrigue to my grownup game of hide and seek.

The next time I passed by the coffee shop, he was sitting by the window wearing an orange polo, khaki shorts, and brown loafers. The less formal attire flattered him well. When our eyes met, he smiled and motioned for me to come inside. I'd imagined our meeting from the first time I saw him but had trouble deciding how to react. I just stood there staring and grinning like I had new dentures before I waved back. I must've looked like a hungry dog salivating over the butcher's best offerings. Good thing I didn't have my tongue hanging out, or he would've thought my name was Lassie. I stared at him until he got up from his table, came outside, and invited me in for coffee. Before I could object, he grabbed my hand and ushered me inside. When he wrapped his hand around mine, I felt a tingly feeling slowly moving up my arm to the center of my chest. I hadn't stuck my finger in an electric socket, I'd just touched him. After we settled into the seats at our table, my initial nervous energy dissipated once I got my breathing under control. I'd been selective with my wardrobe, even though I wasn't guaranteed an audience with the captivating stranger. My thin blue shirt was unbuttoned just enough for the top of my cleavage to hint at what lay beneath the cotton barrier. The amount of leg exposed by my denim mini skirt completed the casual, sexy vibe.

After he'd placed my order, he said, 'So, tell me your name."

"Grace Peterson. And yours?"

"Carter Mann. Nice to meet you, Grace."

"I've seen you in here a couple of times. What brings you to this particular coffee shop?"

"I have consulting clients in the area and stopped here one day between appointments. Now, I come in here whenever I get a chance. This is the best coffee in town. Do you work nearby?"

"No, I'm a third-year nursing student. I come here sometimes to get away from campus and my roommates. And you're right, they have great coffee."

Our words flowed freely once we found our conversational rhythm. His silky voice was liquid stimulation to my ears, and his face delighted my eyes. His bold laughter, smooth tone, and self-assured delivery could've made the word vomit seem sexy. I didn't care what he said as long as I could watch his luscious lips move. Mental checkmarks were made as we discussed future dreams and current marital status. Carter seemed to fit all the requirements on my ideal man checklist. Bonus points for having beautiful teeth.

Carter possessed a magical and alluring charm that left me spellbound. I was hooked on the sensuality that dripped from his being. As if a magnet was pulling me in his direction, I couldn't control the urges I felt in his presence. My endorphins went into overdrive and caused my pleasure centers to become quite active. Thank God I was sitting on the opposite side of the table. He couldn't feel the heat emanating from my body or detect the smell of lust. Several cups of coffee and a muffin later, I declined his offer to take me home. My body and nerves couldn't have handled being alone in a confined space with him. Besides, I didn't know him well enough to risk my safety with a stranger, no matter how good he smelled or how loudly the voices inside my head urged me to take a chance. Once we'd exchanged numbers, I told myself that if he was really interested, we'd see each other again. With my back turned to him, I was grinning so hard my cheeks ached. But I was happy. He was definitely interested in me. Three weeks and four phone calls later, we had our first official date. Mission accomplished

Chapter Five

Third Wheel

Details about our first date were shared with my room-mates as soon as I walked through the door. I was happy to report that he was a perfect gentleman from the beginning of the date to the end. His attentiveness made me feel special the entire evening. He met me in front of the new restaurant by the river, the perfect choice for a first date. Over dinner, we couldn't take our eyes off each other. He complimented me often and made me blush when he talked about the way I looked, the way my eyes sparkled in the ambient light, and the way my radiant smile warmed the room. I felt the same magnetic tension I did in the coffee shop. I couldn't deny the physical attraction building the more I listened to his voice. If eyes were hands, I could've been accused of illegal touching. After dinner, we strolled along the river before he walked me back to my car. It seemed natural when he pulled me into his arms. The sensation of our first kiss made my tongue happy. I was dizzy with desire and lust in his embrace. It was everything I'd imagined the first day I saw him sitting in the coffee shop. After describing the perfect date with the potential catch of the year, one of my roommates said, "Does he have a brother? If so, give him my number."

When the laughter died down, my best friend, AJ, said, "Take your time, Grace. This was just the first date. Everybody tries to look good on the first date. Give it some time before you order wedding invitations."

"Nobody's ordering them, yet, but I really have a good feeling about him."

"Don't think you're the only one that spotted him sitting in that coffee shop. Are you sure he's single? And if he is, have you asked yourself why?"

"Like I said, this was just the first date. I will find out more about him as time goes on."

Once we made our relationship exclusive, Carter visited often. For months he complained about our lack of privacy because of my roommates. When I told AJ about Carter's offer to pay for an apartment for me, she expressed concerns.

"Grace, he's moving way too fast. I don't think this is a good idea."

"Why not? He said he wants to spend more time alone with me. It's hard to do that here."

"Because you haven't known him long enough. I know it sounds good, but something like this always comes with strings attached. I think you should stay here with us. Besides, I'd miss you if you moved out."

"AJ, I'm not leaving town, I'd only be ten minutes away."

"How will you explain this move to your parents?"

"He told me not to tell them he's paying for it. If they ask, I'll let them think it was a special grant or a student loan from the university."

"You would lie to your parents about this man? Grace, this isn't you."

"AJ, please be happy for me. I really think Carter and I can have something special."

"I can't believe you're willing to change who you are for someone you haven't known six months yet? Grace, I really want this to work out for you. Truth be told, I'd probably want to move to. I know it's pointless to try to talk you out of this because you've already made up your mind. I want you to be happy, but I also want you to keep your eyes open."

When Carter moved me into a condo at the end of my junior year, checkmarks were placed beside commitment, kindheartedness, and financial stability. Having my own place was great for our relationship. We spent a significant amount of time together when he wasn't working, and I wasn't studying. To his disappointment, sex was not immediate. I made him work for it. The sage words of my mother kept reminding me of the cows and free milk adage. I was in control of my own body and became an expert at the peekaboo game I played by only exposing strategic parts of myself like a trained fan dancer. I remained in control of how deeply he fondled my body and when to push him away. I came to understand that I was sitting on a gold mine. He had to play by my rules if he wanted my treasure.

As much as Carter protested, his actions indicated he loved the chase. Between all the words and declarations came tangible expressions of his affection. Dinners, promises, and small gifts progressed to shopping sprees, car payments, and weekend getaways. He couldn't buy my body, but how he generously decorated it with clothing and jewelry met no objections. Carter understood he had to make me feel safe and valued before we progressed to a physical union. A connection at a level deeper than his tongue, fingers, and genital parts could reach was a requirement.

Carter continued to give me a prelude of the pleasure that awaited me when I decided to gift him with my treasure. Many times, I pulled away from him, afraid to end the hunt too early. When I could no longer resist his touch, I entrusted my entire body to Carter. Feelings of complete surrender washed over me when I allowed his firm but gentle hands-free reign. He handled my body as if he thought

17

I'd break. I'd never felt so special in any of my other relationships. As we lay together in breathless contentment, he promised many things that made my head spin in anticipation of our continued growth as an exclusive couple. I was in love with Carter Mann.

My love for Carter made it easy for him to talk me into and out of almost anything he wanted. That included my dorm room, time with friends and family, my studies, my underwear, and my mind. My naiveté and his control suited him. The deeper we got into our relationship, the more I began to change into who he wanted me to be. He picked out my wardrobe, hairstyles, and hair color. He took me on shopping sprees but only purchased garments he approved. He was helping me prepare for the business world after graduation, so I didn't mind seeing a more polished version of myself. I felt special that he cared enough to consider my future.

In my eyes, Carter exceeded all expectations from my partner checklist and provided me with more than I'd ever wished for. He was opening a new world for me. In his world, there was status, security, access, money, and a great future. Since he was sharing some of those things with me, how could I refuse to meet his needs? Without hesitation, I did whatever it took to keep his attention. I rationalized that the perks I gained were worth some of the small concessions becoming his woman entailed. I didn't object to changing subtle habits in the progression of our happiness.

Even though a distant concept, when Carter brought up his ideas about marriage, I was all ears. Although he spoke in generality about timing, he was oddly specific about the components of an ideal wife. His wife would look and act a certain way. Her demeanor would be quiet and her tone respectful. Since she would be well taken care of, his wife wouldn't have to work. Her job would involve taking care of the home and giving her full support to him. She would keep their marital business private, and above all else, she would never embarrass him in public. Those concepts seemed a bit primitive for such a refined, progressive, business professional. It sounded like he was looking for a Stepford wife. I had to decide if I was willing to go that far to become Mrs. Mann.

Living without roommates was lonely when Carter was away for work. I hadn't talked to him for a couple of days and was excited when the phone rang. I was all smiles when I answered it with, "Hey baby." When a female voice responded, I thought for sure it was a wrong number. She started calmly but changed her tone the deeper we got into the conversation. I patiently confirmed I wasn't Carter's business associate, cousin, mother, intern, or travel agent. Who was this person and why was she questioning my identity?

Finally, I interrupted her mid-sentence and asked, "Excuse me, but who are you?"

When the words "his fiancé" reached my ear, I almost dropped the phone. When my mind fully comprehended the gravity of her words, my heart cracked.

I wasn't sure I could believe what she said, so I asked, "Since when?"

"Two carats ago," she said. I could hear the smile on her face in her voice.

"Really?" I said before slowly sitting down on the sofa.

"Yes," she replied. "We've been engaged for nine months. It looks like you're dating my fiancé, and I'm asking you nicely to leave him alone."

"Are you sure you're calling about the right man?"

"Yes, he has a crescent-shaped birthmark on his hand and a scar on the inside of his left leg."

Those words hung in the air like the smell of burnt popcorn. Both marks were as described. When I computed how long we'd been together, it coincided with their engagement. I felt my treasure box had been prematurely opened. She'd beat me to the prize. Nowhere on my perfect man checklist did I include a fiancé. Love triangles were not for me. One of us had to go, and I didn't intend for it to be me. I hoped she was ready for a fight.

As usual, Carter returned from his business trip with flowers in hand and a smile planted on his face. I met him at the door with questions about a woman who professed to be his fiancé, a detailed recitation of our conversation, my pent-up anger, and the carefully placed smell of his favorite cologne. I listened to his carefully crafted distortion of facts, not believing any of them. He wasn't annoyed by my concerns about the woman he supposedly dated before we became an exclusive couple. He blamed the call on her inability to accept their break-up. I knew he was lying but didn't care. I didn't have to pretend I believed every word he said. When Carter pulled me into his arms and kissed me, my body quickly responded. I missed him terribly, and he smelled so good when the heat of our bodies connected. I was intent on not letting anything interfere with our time together.

I proceeded with my plan in stealth mode, waiting strategically for my opportunity to eliminate the competition. He was her fiancé, not mine, and they weren't married yet. I wasn't going to make it easy for either of them. I was determined to hold on to my piece of him until he was forced to decide. Because I wouldn't be happy in my current role as an extra, I was willing to become who and what he wanted me to be. As long as I kept him happy, I would remain an option.

While I loved so many things about Carter, his temper was the one thing I never got used to. He could go from zero to one hundred on the anger scale in a split second. It had to be his way or no way. It was on full display the night he came home early from a business trip, and my girlfriends were at the apartment. As soon as he walked through the door and saw my friends, we all saw the disapproving look on his face. He grunted the word "Hello," that sounded more like "Get Out" as he walked past everyone and went into the bedroom. The wine, music, and small talk were no match for his mood-killing aura that poisoned the atmosphere. Our girl's night came to an abrupt end. Although I tried not to show it, I was so embarrassed.

AJ rolled her eyes and said, "Looks like somebody's in trouble. Come on y'all. It's time to go."

The scowl that occupied his face when he first arrived didn't leave when my friends did. I'd barely closed the door before Carter came from the bedroom and said, "Grace, why were those people here?"

"People? Those "people" are my friends. It's not like you don't know any of them. You've known them almost as long as you've known me. We've even had dinner with my best friend, AJ, and her boyfriend several times. What's the problem?"

"You know I value our private time together. That's the main reason I moved you into this apartment."

"I know, but you weren't supposed to be back until tomorrow."

"It doesn't matter when I get here. I should never have to compete with someone else for your attention, especially since I pay all the bills around here."

"Just because you pay for this apartment doesn't mean you own me. I don't want you to ever forget that. I was perfectly fine living with roommates. I moved in here because of you!" I stomped into the bedroom, grabbed my suitcases, and gathered an arm full of garments from my closet.

Carter came into the room and said, "What are you doing, Grace?"

"Leaving, so you can have YOUR apartment back! You've made it clear that it belongs to you and you get to call the shots about who and what is allowed in here. How was I supposed to know you were coming back early? Those are my friends, and you made them, and me feel so uncomfortable."

"I'm sorry for what I said, Grace. I'm tired and I over-reacted."

When Carter grabbed my arm and twisted it behind my back, clothes fell to the floor.

"Stop, Carter, you're hurting me."

"If you listen to me, Grace, I'll let go."

"If you don't let go now, I'm gonna scream." My tone and delivery caught his attention. When he released his grip and backed away, I said, "What is wrong with you? If you don't leave right now, I will."

"Okay, Grace, I'm leaving. I'm so sorry. I really didn't mean to hurt you. I'll call you tomorrow."

I'd never seen that side of him. His actions left me bruised and a bit frightened. The next day, he surprised me with a diamond bracelet. Although it didn't help the swelling go down, it looked good on my wrist and made me feel his apology was sincere. He promised he'd never do that again. Because I was a lovesick fool, I believed him and forgave all.

Carter remained true to his words, and though he raised his voice at me a few times, he kept his hands to himself. I knew my hard work was paying off when he told me he loved me. One day I caught myself looking down at the spot where I imagined my engagement ring would go. No less than three carats would do. If things between us continued to progress, it would be there soon. Three months after the first of many phone calls from his alleged fiancé, she stopped calling. Carter had chosen me. He honored his commitment with a four-carat, pear-shaped engagement ring. I no longer needed to worry about the competition or my checklist. I'd won the prize. All was right with my world.

Rite of Passage

Carter's proposal got me one step closer to having the happily ever after I'd dreamed about as a child. Before we made any wedding plans, I required that he get my father's approval. When he asked my father for my hand in marriage, my parents' reactions differed—elation engulfed my mother, and apprehension radiated from my father. The 4-carat engagement ring's sparkle couldn't remove the furrowed brow or doubt in my father's eyes. Initially, he wasn't as sold on Carter as we were. Since we'd been together for over a year, hopefully, his feelings had changed.

When Carter first met my family, things didn't go as we planned. He made dinner reservations at the best restaurant in town and paid for everything. He tipped the scales toward my father not liking him when he changed my dinner selection. After I shared my preference with everyone, Carter said, "Grace, you ordered that last time. Why not expand your palate? I'll order something different for you."

Immediately, I looked over at my father, who'd cocked his head to one side and frowned as he looked from me to Carter. My mother noticed his response and gently patted him on the arm before his true feelings spewed in our direction. For the remainder of the evening, my father was intent on learning as much as he could about Carter. The information chess match continued between the two men as conversations shifted from his education, career, sports, and current events to Carter's family. I was proud of how he held his own with my father. He kept his answers succinct, and his expression placid. It felt like I was in the middle of a Perry Mason episode. At any moment, I expected a private investigator to walk over to our table with Carter's complete dossier. When we could, my mother and I interjected random quips to lighten the conversation and shift the mood. The temporary truce lasted until dessert.

As my mother and I looked over the dessert menu, Carter said, "After such a big meal, are you sure you need that dessert, Grace?" I was too embarrassed to keep looking at the menu.

My father looked at Carter, then winked at me and said, "Dessert isn't something anyone needs but should never go without."

Needless to say, the evening didn't end on a high note, but the cheesecake was wonderful.

When I visited with my father three days later, I said, "Well, daddy, what did you think of Carter?"

"Do you really want to know?"

"Of course."

"Not sure about him yet, baby girl. Since when did you start letting anybody tell you what to eat and how much? Me and your mother have been married for over thirty years. If I'd ever tried to tell her what to put in her mouth, I wouldn't have had anything to put in mine. What was that all about?"

"Nothing, daddy. He was just getting me to try new things. What's so wrong with that?"

"As long as that's all there is to it, nothing. Until you tell me otherwise, I'll leave it alone, but I'm gonna keep my eye on him.

"Why do you say that?"

"He reminds me of my Uncle Charles, a real lady's man before and after he got married. He was always mean to his wife and had trouble keeping his hands to himself when he got angry. That's what cowards do. The way I was raised, no man should ever put his hands on a woman, period."

I rolled my eyes and said to myself, "How many more times do I have to hear about your Uncle Charles? He's dead."

"And another thing, when Carter wasn't trying to tell you what to eat, he was trying too hard to be impressive and came off as arrogant. He made it a point to tell us about his diversified portfolio and how much real estate he owned. People who got money don't see the need to let everybody know."

"Oh daddy, he's just proud that his hard work paid off. He owns a successful business and is planning for the future. I'm proud of him. You, of all people, know how hard it is to own your own business. Give him a chance."

"Grace, I want you to be careful. Glass shines just like diamonds, but they're not the same. What you see from far off can sometimes fool you."

I loved my daddy and was grateful that he was so protective when it came to me and my sister, but my heart knew what was best for me. I followed its lead and continued my love affair with Carter. Twelve months after meeting my parents, we were seeking their approval of our marriage. Obtaining my college degree was my father's main concern. Graduation, then marriage, was the promise I made to my parents. I could still see the hesitation in my father's eyes when he looked from Carter to me. I'd be crushed if he didn't approve. He turned to me and asked, "Is this really what you want?"

"Yes, daddy."

"I'm not ready to let you go yet. You're my baby."

"I'll always be your baby, daddy."

"You're right about that. I also know that once you make your mind up to do something, it's pointless to try to stop you. That's always been a blessing and a curse for you. When you were about five years old, you tried to climb over the fence and go to your friend's house. Even though we told you to stay in the yard, you were determined to go anyway. When we looked out the kitchen window, your t-shirt had gotten caught on the wooden slat, and you were two feet off the ground, arms flailing, yelling for help. All I could say was, "Headstrong, just like me."

I remembered that incident well. My parents were laughing so hard, and they didn't have the heart to punish me.

"You're a grown woman, Grace, and grown folks always find ways to do whatever they want, regardless of what anybody says. It looks like your mind and your heart are too far gone for me to try to get in your way."

I acknowledged his insight with a smile. As he held my hands, I saw love in his eyes.

Then he turned to Carter and said, "All I ask is that you treat her right."

"I will, sir, I love Grace. You have my word on that."

My father took my hands and placed them in Carter's. We both breathed a sigh of relief when he said, "You have my blessing. Now I want you to understand something, Carter. Grace is my child, not yours. She's yours to love, not to raise. We've already done that."

Carter had a puzzled look on his face. He didn't understand his comments.

My father continued, "If you ever get to the point where you feel you want to put your hands on her, you send her back to me."

"Yes, sir, I understand," was all Carter said.

I remember thinking, "Too late. That's in the past. The bruised wrist already healed. Carter already said he was sorry. He's not your Uncle Charles."

Shortly after we picked a date, Carter asked my parents to let him pay for the entire wedding. Although it was a wonderful gesture, they refused. I believed my father could read the joy in my eyes with that decision. I was a daddy's girl, and I wanted that tradition to remain with my family. When we discussed Carter's offer privately as a family, my father commented that I was his baby girl, and he didn't want to feel as if he was selling me to the highest bidder. My father was a proud man who believed in taking care of his own. I loved my father even more for letting me know that he'd do anything in his power to make my dreams come true.

Chapter Seven

Generational Wisdom

Our wedding was scheduled for October, five months after I received my nursing degree. The closer the wedding day came, the harder it was to juggle my time between Carter, school, and finalizing wedding plans. I found myself sacrificing one priority for another. Carter saw the stress I was under and encouraged me to consider taking some time off from school at the end of the semester. I could always go back once we got married. I strongly considered that option but wouldn't decide until I talked to my parents. One of my father's concerns about my getting engaged was my education. I'd promised him I wouldn't get married until I had my degree in hand. I didn't know how I could go back on my word. But what Carter said made so much sense. I was struggling to keep everything together.

I decided to speak with my mother about my situation and a solution during our traditional Christmas dinner prep. She was the easy one. I surmised that if I got her on my side, together we could convince my father to see things our way.

"Mom, I need your advice."

"I'm listening."

"I'm thinking about dropping out of college for a semester."

"This close to the end? I hope you realize how hard it is to go back once you walk away. What brought that about?"

"Everything is so hard for me right now. I've got too much going on."

She looked me straight in the eyes and said, "There's more to it than that. I can see it in your eyes. What's going on, Grace?"

"Carter and I were talking, and he said he makes enough to take care of me. Since I won't have to work, he doesn't think I need the degree. I could devote more time to planning our wedding, looking for a place big enough for both of us, and spending more time with him. Maybe I could even travel with Carter and get a glimpse of what my life will be like after we're married. I can always go back to school, just not now. I need a break."

My mother kept stirring the food in the pots and said, "All I've heard you consider was what Carter wanted. I haven't heard anything about what would be best for you, Grace."

My mother giggled and said, "To be young and in love. I remember what those days were like when your father started courting me. I was just as foolish as an alcoholic with a bottle of liquor. I believed I was in control. That couldn't' have been farther from the truth. I think you're tipsy right now and what I'm telling you is gonna go in one ear and out the other. You can't be held responsible for not retaining this wisdom right now. You're in love and planning a wedding. Your mind is up in the clouds. Hopefully, some of it will find its way back to you when you need it."

"Alright. I get it, mom. Tell me how you really feel."

"Since you asked. I'll tell you. Now, when it comes to school, my advice is to get your degree."

"But I won't need it. I won't have to work after we're married."

"I see. Grace, my mother gave me some advice that was passed down from her mother. Now that you're getting married, I think it's time to pass it down to you." She said, "*Even if you don't have to use your degree, always have a way to take care of myself. Don't sit around and wait for a man to give you things. He will only give you what he thinks you ought to have. That keeps you under his control. Losing control comes slowly. You hardly know it's happening.*" "I've never felt helpless, and I don't want that for you."

"I don't think Carter is trying to control me. He's not like that. He just wants what's best for me."

"Life is full of surprises. You can't plan it like you planned your wedding. It doesn't work like that. Marriage gets hard sometimes. I just want you to be prepared for when the honeymoon is over and real-life settles in."

"Yes, ma'am. I think we'll be fine. We love each other, and he makes me happy. I want to make Carter happy too. Isn't that what matters most?"

"Don't miss what I'm saying, Grace. I encourage you to love your husband deeply, but don't lose the essence of who you are. If you don't know who you are, how can you add to someone else's life? You can be all of you and part of him at the same time. Don't forget that you are still a complete person. I don't care what that preacher tells you about becoming one." My mother chuckled before she said, "Try to cross your fingers on that part when you say your vows!"

We both burst into laughter. I understood that my mother was just trying to love me. I appreciated her wisdom and good intentions. We hugged each other tightly before she took off her apron and sat down.

"Come here, baby, and sit with me. After you're a married woman, I won't get to do this."

Just as I did when I was a child, I sat down on her lap. As she rocked me back and forth, I said, "I love you, Mommy."

"I love you too, Grace."

I had such clarity after my conversation with my mother. I'd made a promise to my parents I intended to fulfill. No matter how hard I thought it would be, I was

30

committed. It was the only way I could be at peace on my wedding day.

The day I received my nursing degree, I was all smiles. I underestimated the satisfaction of completing something for myself that I, and my parents, could be proud of. The pride in my parent's eyes when I walked across the stage humbled me. It showed a depth of love I hoped to emulate as a parent. I understood how much they'd sacrificed for me and didn't want to trivialize their expression of love. Had I not completed my educational aspirations, I wouldn't have witnessed their joy. I understood how my degree was being held by those who weren't fortunate enough to attend college but encouraged others to seek greatness. It would've been a slap in their faces to have squandered their dreams. I thanked God for the gifts of wisdom from my elders.

Chapter Eight

With This Ring

The stifling heat of the summer was replaced by the freshness of October air and helped cool down the remaining remnants of the summer's heat. It was the perfect time for a wedding. There were so many last-minute things to get done but with the help of family and friends, everything was beautiful. Colorful leaves served as the perfect backdrop for the change occurring in my life. It was my wedding day. Like the leaves of fall, our lives were changing forever. I saw a world full of expectations waiting for me with the man I loved. I was becoming a wife and, hopefully, someday a mother. My life would be perfect. All my dreams were coming true, starting with Carter, the man I adored.

The pre-wedding rituals were a blur. One minute I was eating breakfast with my family, the next minute I was at the church with bridesmaids in coordinated dresses and my maid of honor helping me into my gown. I was overcome with emotions after my mother zipped up my gown and our eyes met in the full-length mirror. We saw the payoff from the three trips it took to find the perfect wedding gown. Its sparkles and lace came to life, from the veil to the train, with the slightest movement. I would always cherish those moments with my sister and mother as we added another layer to the bond we shared.

As beautiful as it was, my dress was upstaged by my mother. It couldn't outshine the beauty I saw in her face.

Her quiet strength nurtured me into the confident woman I was that day. As much as it was my wedding day, it was a celebration of the woman I'd become because of her. My dress would be worn once and carefully packed away, but she would continue to be part of my life

My father entered my dressing room right before it was time for the ceremony to begin. My mother and I shared one final moment before she gave me time alone with him. I saw the love in his eyes when he said, "You look beautiful, Grace. I can't believe my baby is getting married. Are you sure you don't want to change your mind?"

I smiled, kissed him on the cheek, and replied, "Not a chance."

"Just say the word, and I'll shut all of this down."

"Would you, Daddy?"

"In a heartbeat," he said before he hugged me one final time and we exited the room. I was ready for my father to gift me to my husband.

When the wedding march began to play, I was a bundle of nerves. I looked at my father and said, "Thank you, daddy." He patted my hand as we both fought hard to hold back the tears. After that day, I would no longer be his baby girl. I would be a married woman. The thought of that thrilled and frightened me. As much as I hated to admit it, things between us would never be the same. He wouldn't be the most important man in my life. Someone else would hold that honor and would have to discover my quirky, complex layers. Carter would get to understand my nervous laughter; that Easter was my favorite holiday; that the tooth fairy always left five dollars; that my sister cut off one of my braids for her doll; that I loved to catch snowflakes on my tongue; that I asked Santa for the dog from the Wizard of Oz; that I loved the beauty and marvel of fireflies. Learning those things about me would make our journey an adventure.

My father kissed me on my cheek, lowered my veil, and extended his right arm. Together we walked down the aisle to my new life. I was ready to become one with Carter and honor our union from that day forward. I'd stick with him and by him through the best of times and the worst of times. I'd be honored to celebrate with him through prosperity, build with him in the face of poverty, spend time with him in good health, and care for him through illness. I was ready to finally be Mrs. Carter Mann and to love him like no other, treasure our shared moments, and stay with him until separated by death. I cried as Carter, and I repeated our vows. I was overjoyed when he declared, "With this ring, I thee wed," as he slid the band on my finger. After we sealed our promises with a kiss, I wanted to jump for joy. He was all mine.

Chapter Nine

Bliss

The first year of our marriage was wonderful. It felt like the honeymoon never ended. We lived our vows and became inseparable. Carter became my everything, and I became absorbed in his wants and needs. My soul got sucked into his, and I didn't know that I could love so deeply or so completely. Although we'd made love before, it was different once we were married. It reminded me of billowing curtains responding to the gentle breeze. Our bodies meshed and the space between us was lost in heavenly passion. Our hearts became one. There was no room for anyone else.

Before we married, Carter traveled extensively for work. That didn't change. Sometimes I traveled with him, often having mini-vacations filled with pampering while he worked and passion when the workday ended. Even with his hectic travel schedule, I didn't feel overlooked or ignored. All my needs were being met, in and out of our marital bed. I was doted on, given what I asked for and more. The epitome of a loving marriage was demonstrated to me by my husband.

I was living the good life until allegations of marital betrayal entered my world. I wasn't prepared for the gut punch to my pride. I was so naïve that I never saw it coming until she called. An anonymous voice broke the news to me about her boyfriend, my husband. Her attack on me was brutal, and we were never close enough to touch. She politely told me my husband gifted her with an STD.

"Liar," I screamed into the phone before I abruptly hung up. I was speechless. That was original. That topic of conversation was a first for me. I wondered what she would try next.

A million thoughts bombarded my mind as I tried to process her unsettling words. My mind tried to invalidate what I heard with the facts as I knew them.

Over the past year, there were times when he didn't pick up the phone when I called. But that was normal. It'd always been like that, even while we were dating. Between the constant traveling and his demanding clients, there would be times when he was unreachable. In context, there was no reason to question his movements. Why should I believe she had my best interests at heart? Surely my husband wouldn't put my health in jeopardy. Besides, I earned a nursing degree. I'd be able to tell if something was wrong.

When I answered the phone again, I heard the same voice.

Her tone was more authoritative when she said, "Don't hang up. I called earlier because we really need to talk."

Not sure if I should continue listening or hang up again, I asked, "Who are you?"

"Does that matter?"

"Not to me. You called me earlier. What do you want?"

"I want you to believe what I told you about your husband."

"And why should I do that?"

"Because it's true! Look, I don't care what you do once I hang up this phone. I did what I thought was decent by letting you know. I'm sure he hasn't told you. I just talked to him and he denied it. If I were in your shoes, I'd make an appointment with my gynecologist and a divorce lawyer."

I couldn't believe the gall of this woman. She was trying to give me marital and medical advice. She didn't even know me and probably didn't know Carter, either.

Before I could respond, she said, "Ask him about Hotel Avery, room 929."

"Click" was the next sound she heard. Since she'd called twice, I was compelled to listen but didn't want to hear any more of her dirty secrets. I didn't want to be challenged by the possibility of her ugly truth. I'd endured her confession with no audible reactions while corroding away on the inside. Now, I wanted to scream. She'd done her job by attempting to dilute the sanctity of our marriage and make me question everything about our commitment. If she couldn't keep him, she would ensure I wouldn't want him.

I didn't believe her. Carter and I were happy. I didn't want to be challenged by the probability of her truth. I couldn't let baseless accusations from a stranger prevail and mess up what we had. Seeds of doubt had been planted but not yet rooted. I had two days before Carter came home to decide whether or not to confront him. If she was right, it would destroy everything. If I wrongly accused him, it would ruin everything. I couldn't risk it. I just wanted my perfect life fantasy to appear attainable as long as I could. I decided to keep her phone call a secret. For now, everything would stay the same.

Chapter Ten

Bugged Out

When Carter finally got home from his business trip, he seemed preoccupied and distant. Our welcome home patterns were altered. He wouldn't let me near him for any length of time. When I slipped into the shower to properly welcome him home, he hugged me briefly then left me standing under the water, naked and alone. That was a first. He uttered something about a delayed flight and an early morning meeting as he exited the shower. He was asleep as soon as his head hit the pillow. Maybe he was just tired.

The next morning, he was gone before I woke up. That night, he greeted me with flowers and the passionate hugs and kisses I didn't get the prior evening. All seemed normal again. After dinner, Carter apologized about needing time to work and went into his office. That gave me time to prepare myself for a romantic evening with my husband. Since I hadn't gotten a bikini wax recently, I opted for some self-help with a razor. I put on his favorite perfume and the most irresistible lingerie I owned. I planned was to lure him away from his office for a different type of work. To my disappointment, he was asleep on the couch when I returned.

Although I'd been happy with the aesthetic outcome, days later, I began to regret using a razor on such a sensitive region of my body. Before I could afford waxes, I groomed my bikini area. I'd almost forgotten the irritation that followed. I couldn't fight the urge to scratch the itch in my pubic region. My amateur grooming caused more irritation than I'd counted on. I knew it would be fine in a couple of days. In the meantime, I indulged in a soothing hot bath for relief.

Sliding down into a steamy, bubbly bath was one of my favorite forms of relaxation. The hotter, the better. With all the abnormal behavior my husband was exhibiting, I needed something to relieve the mental and physical tension. My mind tried to entertain the words from a faceless confession as the reason for his uncharacteristic behavior. I banished those thoughts into isolation. I didn't want to lend credibility to the words of someone looking to disrupt our marriage. I willed my mind to only think about the night I had planned for later.

I closed my eyes and let the clean scents and steam fill my nostrils. When I opened my eyes, a dark object was floating toward me on a fluffy peak of white suds. Its dark body stood out against the sea of aqua. From beneath the object, my finger lifted it and brought it closer to my face. It moved. So, did I. I screamed and plunged my hand deep into the ocean of scented water. Whatever was on my finger was gone. I nearly lost my footing as I scrambled to get out of the tub. After I'd wrapped myself in a towel, I looked back at the water. There were more dark objects floating around. I grabbed a tissue and collected the specimen. When I brought it into view, I saw a live insect. To my horror and disgust, I had pubic lice. I'd been bugged. Thinking about those living insects eating away at the most private part of my body made me gag. I counted my blessings that it wasn't herpes but wished he'd given me flowers instead.

I sat down on the toilet seat and internalized what that meant. Skin to skin contact was the only way to end up with those gifts. It didn't take a college degree to determine how I became infested. I was forced to acknowledge the veracity of the message from the anonymous caller from room 929 of Hotel Avery. Everything about the last few days, the call from the stranger, the elusive actions of my husband, and the itching in my genital area, made sense. I was ashamed of the facts that Carter nor I could deny. My perfect marital image had been shattered in front of someone else.

My immediate focus was to eliminate my clingy friends. I felt dirty. I wanted to shave off all the hair on my body below my waist. As conclusive as that methodology would have been, it would have caused more itching. That was not an ideal solution. I would have to self-medicate until my medical condition improved but had to be careful as I searched for the proper medication. My dignity was at stake. I drove to the next town over, too afraid someone I knew would recognize me. I visited several stores before I felt comfortable enough to make my purchase. I scanned the parking lot and counted the number of cars. Fewer cars meant fewer eyes to critique and criticize my purchase. I wouldn't be able to withstand another blow to my emotional foundation if someone else found out about my minor medical condition. I was too humiliated to look at the clerk as she handed me my change and a bag full of items used to mask my true purpose. On the way home, the overwhelming desire to scratch myself returned. I felt like a dog with fleas. I needed to eliminate the issue as quickly as possible. Then, I wanted to kill Carter.

Chapter Eleven

Gift Exchange

Once home, I became my own triage nurse. I had to switch from patient to professional. Since I already had a diagnosis, I administered treatment. The patient in me wanted to scream as I lifted the insects from my body with a tiny comb. All that was left was to trim the area as closely as possible, shave my legs and thighs, and take another hot bath. The professional in me remained calm and retained some specimens for later. Since he'd surprised me, I felt obliged to surprise him with unexpected gifts.

After dinner, I went into the bedroom and prepared for my version of a lie-detector test. I walked up behind Carter, smelling of his favorite perfume, wearing a bathrobe and thong, and started massaging his shoulders. I leaned into him until my breasts touched the back of his head, while my hands slowly moved from his shoulders to his chest. I whispered in his ear, "It's been a long time. I'm ready for bed. Aren't you?"

"Not now, Grace. I've got too much work to do."

I walked around in front of him, opened my bathrobe, and asked, "Can't it wait?"

His eyes widened, but he made no movements toward me. I could see he was tempted but remained glued to his chair. His actions were abnormal for his carnal appetite. As much as I wanted to remain in denial, he was confessing without saying a word.

Determination for a confession inspired me to start giving him a lap dance. I snuggled my breasts into his face while my hands roamed his body. His physical reaction contradicted his words. When I tried to place his hand inside my thong, he jerked it away, stood up, and said, "That's enough, Grace."

My heart sank. His behavior told me that he already knew what he'd done to me. How ironic that I was married before I ever got an STD.

"Is something wrong, Carter? Why won't you touch me?"

He wouldn't answer. I reached into the pocket of my robe, pulled out a Ziploc bag and said, "Are you afraid of these bugs you gifted me with? Are you afraid I would give them back to you?"

All he said was, "I don't know what you're talking about." His response was remarkably inconsistent for my demeanor and behavior. If he'd accused me of giving him an STD, I would be screaming my innocence at the top of my lungs.

"What the hell, Carter? That's all you can come up with!" I threw the gift bag at him and said, "I think these belong to you."

He looked down at the bag by his feet and said, "I have no idea what this is all about."

"You knew you had a disease, and you didn't have the decency to tell me."

"You think I gave you an STD? No way," he said as he shook his head in denial.

I couldn't find the words to respond. All I could think about was that I was an SDW with an STD, a Sexually Disappointed Wife with a Sexually Transmitted Disease. My faithfulness to our vows meant nothing to him. Neither did my condition. His facial expression never changed after I waved the bag in front of his face.

"What have you been doing while I was away? Did you spend the night with your sister? You know how she is."

The more he talked, the angrier I got.

"You've got the nerve to put this on me? My sister? Don't you want to know how I found out? She called me."

"Who called you?"

"The woman you've been trading bugs with."

"Ok, that's enough, Grace. You're becoming hysterical and irrational. You need to calm down."

"No, it's not enough. It won't be enough until you admit what you did. Be a man, Carter. You did this, now own your truth."

"Like I said, I don't know what you're talking about, Grace."

At the top of my voice, I yelled, "You're a dirty, stinking, adulterous, liar!"

Carter didn't say another word. The back of his hand against my cheek spoke for him. I landed in a heap on the floor. He stepped over me, went to our bedroom and slammed the door. I picked myself up from the floor and took my stinging face and broken ego into the guest bedroom. I locked the door, sat on the bed, and keeled over in total disbelief. When my head hit the pillow, so did the tears.

I wanted so badly to call my father. Fear for my husband kept me from following through. I'd witnessed my father's protective side emerge when my sister's boyfriend cursed at her in front of him. He said, "Son, you don't know who you're messing with. If you don't leave my house right now, I will cut you five ways; quick, deep, hard, long, and often." I couldn't imagine what he would want to do to Carter. He cheated on me, gave me a disease, and hit me in my face. There was no one I could talk to about my problem. I'd have to figure it out on my own.

Chapter Twelve

Healing

I couldn't go out of the house until the swelling in my face went down. I couldn't get away from that moment. Each time I looked in the mirror, my swollen face rekindled feelings of humiliation I tried to forget. I was reminded of what we lost that day. My complete trust in my husband was eroded. It was apparent there were character flaws he concealed while we were dating. A frightening question entered my mind. What kind of person had I married?

For more than a week, we barely spoke. We moved in measured silence. Neither of us wanted to disturb the currents of distrust stored in layers just beneath the surface. I kept waiting for some sign of remorse from him. The longer I waited, the more evident it became he never would admit the affair. I wanted him to understand my feelings. Just because he was finished with the lie and the betrayal didn't mean I was. I was disappointed, but I was also hurt. The disappointment faded away, but the hurt lingered. It was deeper than I could express or his eyes could see. I couldn't figure out why he chose to stray away from the marriage. I was giving him everything he needed. Two short years of marital bliss didn't seem long enough for the itch to occur. What happened? It was five years too soon.

The nights I slept alone gave me the time and space to consider what would be best for me. I had to make a monumental decision, but my elevated emotional state kept me confused. I questioned if he would lose respect for me if there were no consequences for his betrayal. I wondered if things would go back to normal or if I would resent him for hurting me. I wasn't sure I needed to flush my marriage down the drain for one mistake. I had to decide if our marriage could survive infidelity and if I was willing to take that chance.

I missed the closeness we shared but was leery about restoring our intimate relationship. Always in the back of my mind was the thought that he may infect me with something more serious next time. Before I would consider sharing our bodies again, I demanded, and he agreed, to prove neither of us had any underlying medical conditions. I didn't need any more clinical surprises. Both Carter and I got clean bills of health. I wasn't surprised by my results but couldn't say the same thing about his. We'd both dodged a bullet shot by his gun of stupidity.

My continued occupation of the guestroom kept my body off-limits. Carter was forced to make efforts toward reconciliation. He started to seduce my mind with increased attention and escalating gifts. He winked at me from across the room and called me throughout the day. Although I wouldn't answer, I smiled when I heard the messages. Carter even cooked dinner one night, something I enjoyed that he hadn't done for me in a long time. It felt good to see him trying to make amends. He went a little too far when he pressed his body against mine while attempting to hug me from behind. I pushed him away and went straight to the spare bedroom. I didn't want to show him how good it felt to have his arms around me again. The next day, he left a hand-written note on my bedroom door. A few days later, chocolate kisses were in the cutlery drawer, and two dozen roses were in my car. The theatre tickets on the kitchen table and my favorite wine in the fridge made me smile, as did the delivery from my favorite dress shop and the bracelet under my pillow. Each time one of those gestures was discovered, the ice around my heart thawed. He was luring me out of the spare bedroom.

I don't believe he ever said he was sorry for his infidelity or the assault. Eventually, I didn't care. I couldn't play the treasure hunt game I mastered while we were dating. We were married, and I immensely enjoyed the conjugal pleasures that were expected and essential to a healthy marriage. He knew that about me and exploited my weakness the night he intentionally bumped against me and grabbed my hand. His lips touched my cheek before placing them on mine. His hands caressed the places on my body that longed for contact and the release of pent-up anxiety and desire. His whispers weakened me until my body betrayed my resolve. It always did whenever he touched me like that. It was like a mild electrical current coursing through my body. Like a magic trick, my clothes disappeared while I was under his spell. His skillful hands smoothed over the hurt and caused my walls to collapse. The floral pattern on the sofa became the field of flowers that encircled our reconciliation. I fully opened my body back up to him in total surrender. Each wave of passion pushed my doubts further and further into the back of my mind. Years later, I'd understand that the decision my body talked me into marked the downfall of my self-respect.

Chapter Thirteen

All Rise

When I last looked at the clock on my nightstand, it was past midnight. When I looked again, it was seven. The alarm produced by the radio announcer's voice highjacked my mind. *"Here's your morning update from the WRPE newsroom. The arraignment for prominent businessman, Carter Mann, is set for today. Mr. Mann, who's been accused of brutally assaulting a pregnant woman, was arrested on Friday. The victim is reportedly in critical but stable condition. After speaking with Mr. Mann's legal counsel, he expects his client to be released on bail today. Mr. Mann has no criminal record and does not pose a flight risk. We will keep you up-to-date on the latest developments with this case."*

After a restless night, those words were the last things I wanted to hear. Carter's arraignment was just a few hours away. It was time to put our marital skeletons back in the closet, or I wouldn't be able to sit in the courtroom in support of my husband. I wondered what his current indiscretion would cost our family. Secret suffering was one thing; being publicly humiliated and ridiculed was insufferable. Maybe our future would look better once Carter came back home. I'd learn the answer in the next hours.

Since Carter was arrested on Friday, he spent the weekend in jail. I had to mentally prepare for the unknown consequences of his day in court. Just as the reporter said, his attorney speculated he'd be released on bail after the arraignment. He prepared us for the possibility of house arrest or electronic monitoring while awaiting trial. We would do whatever was necessary to get him released. Once home, we'd have a lot to discuss. I'd be mindful of my words as I sought answers to questions that ate away at me. He'd already be agitated by the public humiliation. I wouldn't increase his shame privately. It would be non-productive and possibly dangerous. First on the list would be the issue of that baby, the one aspect of the whole ordeal that pained me the most. If it was his child, I feared adding that load would break me. I'd already put up with so much over the years. The baby couldn't be my burden to carry. I had enough baggage of my own.

As I got closer to the courthouse, I was haunted by a violent encounter with Carter that ended in the loss of my first child. He cried tears of regret in the aftermath of what he'd done. He didn't know I was pregnant when he kicked me in the back and caused me to fall. It was a small consolation for me but an entirely different situation for his accuser. She was near the end of her pregnancy when he allegedly attacked her. No way he wasn't aware of the potential trauma that he could cause. I fully understood the reason for his charges. He'd gone too far. No one would be as forgiving as I'd been.

Walking into a courtroom was my watershed moment. My appearance there was long overdue and far from what I'd expected. Absent were darkly colored wood panels as the backdrop for the elevated throne of justice. The modern version of our local courtroom had lighter wood tones, didn't feel as stuffy but retained the formality. The person who could change lives with one bang of a gavel would still sit high above all others. Instead of reverent silence, the room was filled with voices that ebbed and flowed while we waited for court to convene. I should've already acquainted myself with the protocols of the judicial system before now. It wasn't as scary as I'd imagined.

Years ago, when I contemplated breaking away from Carter's abuse, I'd looked at it as a place that could possibly rob me of my self-esteem, lifestyle, and privacy. There were things that even my parents didn't know about, and I wanted to keep it that way. I didn't want to be publicly humiliated by airing my marital secrets to anyone who happened to be within earshot. I'd never know how different my life would have been had I spoken up just once. My choice to remain silent about his abuse meant more suffering, but I needed some small part of my dignity to remain in place as my anchor. I couldn't lose everything or appear as if I was begging for support from a man who appeared to despise my presence. How sobering that another woman caused me to be in the courtroom because of his abuse. No doubt, our stories overlapped with common fears, scars, and pain. When it was all said and done, I wondered what else she would force me to do.

I watched as Carter was paraded into court in jailhouse garments, accented by silver bracelets similar to the ones he adorned on our front porch. They still seemed to fit him nicely. When Carter saw me, he smiled as he sat with his attorney, waiting for his case to be called. He seemed genuinely happy to see me. That felt good. I returned the smile but didn't move any other part of my body.

I observed the game of courtroom musical chairs as inmates were guided up to and away from the judge. No one was fighting for their seat in the spotlight. After a short time, I became familiar with the arraignment procedures. I'd been waiting for about an hour when the clerk called out the name Carter Mann, aka Ben Wilson. I watched intently as Carter took his turn in the game. We were prepared for an extremely high bail amount. We didn't care. I was willing to pay any amount to secure his temporary freedom, no matter how many assets we had to liquidate. We had a plan in place. Unfortunately, we overlooked the plans of the prosecutor. I got an uneasy feeling in the pit of my stomach as she presented facts about Carter's case. The inflection in her voice as she referenced the heinous nature of the crime was troubling. Despite the vehement pleadings of his attorney, the decision of the judge was final. There would be no bail— more fodder for the evening news cycle.

Carter's body language showed extreme frustration as he looked from his attorney to the judge. And just like that, the gavel banged again, and the bailiff ushered him back out of the courtroom through the same door as the others. He looked back over his shoulder at me before he disappeared from sight. His turn in the game was over. He didn't win. I was glad no one knew I was there supporting Carter. I hoped I'd appeared to be a casual onlooker who was just as upset about the charges levied against the accused, my husband. There's no telling what they would have said about me had they known my true identity. I questioned whether I should have attended court in a wig and sunglasses.

I was crushed. I needed time to process the decision of the judge. I didn't expect that outcome today. I wouldn't need the power of attorney or the name of the bail bondsman I had in my purse. I thought we would be home in time for dinner with a list of stipulations associated with his release, maybe even an electronic monitor. I was disappointed. The "no bail" outcome meant I would be alone for a long time. Our honest conversation would have to wait.

Chapter Fourteen

Promises, Promises

When I exited the courtroom and waited in the lobby for Carter's attorney, another woman exited at the same time. I couldn't shake the feeling that she was watching me. She lingered around outside for a moment before she stepped into the elevator and disappeared beyond the slow-moving doors. Although we never spoke, her presence made me uncomfortable. Carter's attorney came up behind me and tapped me on the shoulder. Good news. I'd get a chance to see my husband before they returned him to his cell. Through the double doors and ten paces down the hallway, we stopped at a room with a guard posted outside. Once inside the room, I fell into Carter's arms. I was a ball of emotions but was glad to be soothed by the touch of my husband, no matter how temporary we both knew it would be. As we hugged, he asked, "Are you ok, Grace?" Tears replaced my words. All I could do was nod before he caressed my face and kissed me. I'd missed him so much and was disappointed with the outcome of the hearing. When our lips met some of the tension left my body. Our attorney cleared his throat and announced he would give us some privacy before leaving us alone in the room.

After we sat down at the table, Carter took my hands in his. The energy in the room shifted when he started to speak. I got a bad feeling in the pit of my stomach. There was more to this show of compassion than genuine concern for me.

"Baby, I need your help. I know you don't understand everything that's going on right now but if you help me, this can all go away. I promise things between us will be different."

My first thoughts were, "Until when? Until you got bored with me again? Your probation was over? Your arrogance took over? You no longer needed me?" I didn't trust the desperation of the person who was addressing me no more than I'd trust a cornered animal. Furthermore, who exactly was I talking to? Was it Ben, Will, Anthony, Jason, Stanley, James, Nick, or Carter asking for my help? Who knows? Undoubtedly, one of those personas needed me. Maybe Carter meant it this time when he promised things would change. I was intrigued by the possibility of stability with my husband, so I asked, "What do you need?"

He looked me in the eyes and said, "We have to do some damage control with these allegations. I'm so sorry to put our family in this situation. Grace, I will make it up to you. I promise. But right now, I need you to talk to Eva."

I was confused, so I asked, "Who's Eva? Is she a witness?"

Carter got up from his seat and walked across the room. When he turned around, he said, "No. She's the woman who had me arrested. She's responsible for the situation we're in."

I dropped my head and sat quietly as my hands played with each other. I wasn't surprised by his relationship with another woman or the fact that he pled not guilty. My gut and his history already told me the assault allegations were warranted. Since he wasn't getting out on bail, I couldn't imagine what he thought I could do. I wouldn't lie to give him an alibi. Carter sat down at the table again and calmed my fidgeting fingers by placing his hands over mine. After a brief pause, he looked me straight in my eyes again and said, "Grace, I need you to convince Eva to drop these charges."

The shock of his request caught me off guard. I pulled my hands from beneath his grasp. If he could've read my troubled eyes, which were probably as big as saucers, they were saying, "Hell no!" I was stunned by his even asking me to do something so degrading. I was repulsed at the thought of confronting that woman in her current state. I knew how it felt to have been on the receiving end of one of his assaults. If he was as angry as I imagined, she would wear his anger marks long past her physical healing.

I closed my eyes and let his request sink in. My hands wouldn't stop searching for places on my face to rest. My fingers made circular movements on my temples, then covered my eyes to relieve the tension of the moment. I was sure they were bulging out of their sockets. Hundreds of thoughts and questions fought for the honor of being said first. "Is that your baby?" won.

Without hesitation, Carter responded, "No. That's not my child. Period."

"And Eva? What did you do to her?"

"We argued. I told her I wasn't leaving you. She didn't like that. Maybe I slapped her once or twice or even pushed her down, but that's no reason for her to do all this to me. To us. Can't you see, she's just mad. Please, baby, talk to her. Woman to woman. I know she will listen to you. Grace, I'm counting on you. Ask her what it would take to end this. Tell her to name her price."

I was torn. Carter sounded so convincing. I wanted to believe him. More than that, I wanted him to need me again. But if he was lying, it would destroy the little piece of hope for our marriage I clung to. How much more of myself was I willing to give up? I started to wonder if he was worth the risk. I feared his freedom from prosecution would mean he wouldn't need me any longer. In the current scenario, he'd placed me in a place of power and respect, though

53

temporary it may have been. I decided to risk everything and agreed to talk to Eva.

We were caught up in a celebratory hug when the attorney returned with a plastic bag filled with Carter's personal belongings. His return meant it was time for Carter to go. My heart sank. Since there would be no bail, he thought the items were safer with me. In our final moments together, Carter pulled me close and whispered in my ear, "Thank you, baby. Please keep this between us."

I nodded in affirmation before I said, "I love you, Carter. I'll see you soon."

Before he let me go and exited the room he said, "I love you, Grace." I was grateful for the uninterrupted time we had to develop a plan for his freedom while we waited for the trial to begin.

Chapter Fifteen

Second Thoughts

When I drove away from the courthouse, I felt validated and important. As much as I hated to admit it, even with the way he'd treated me in the past, I knew I would do whatever he wanted. I always did what it took to hold on to our marriage. Divorce would've been considered a failure. This time, my husband needed me to confront his current mistress. I'd briefly felt sorry for his accuser when the court clerk read Carter's charges because I'd experienced that angry, ugly side of my husband. After speaking with him, I quarantined any notions of empathy. There was no time or tolerance for that. I had to save my husband.

The radio announcer's voice filled the air with melodies of reality that challenged my feelings about an executable plan for Carter's release. *"Late-breaking news from the WRPE newsroom. Prominent businessman Carter Mann was arraigned today on charges of aggravated domestic assault and assault against a fetus. His petition for bail was denied. Mr. Mann will remain in jail until trial. Stay tuned to WRPE for further details as they become available."*

I turned off the radio and rode home in silence. It felt like I'd been slapped in the face. Once I had the time and space to think without the pressure of his presence and the weight of his desperation, doubt began to crowd out the feelings of euphoria I'd experienced earlier. I'd been caught up in the moment and forgot to consider life once the feel of his hugs and the sound of his pleading faded away. I never considered how quickly reality would set in. It was a thirty-minute drive from the courthouse to my home. I was still five minutes away.

The more I thought about going to see Eva, the more uneasy I became. Helping Carter meant I'd have to confront a battered woman in her hospital bed. I didn't have to pretend why I consented to his request. We both knew how desperate I was for his love. He'd dangled the carrot of reconciliation and a fresh start in front of me, and I was willing to follow it mindlessly into possible self-destruction and disappointment. My husband was cunning and always said exactly what I wanted to hear. In the face of our history, his words began to ring hollow. It appeared he would be my consolation prize since his pool of prospective suitors would drop tremendously after this type of public exposure. Once I brought the reclaimed gift home, would I still be happy with it? Sadly, the answer would probably be "no."

My mind groaned with regret. What he wanted was too unkind to me and to the woman he assaulted. How would I find the courage to ask her not to do something I should've done years ago? I didn't think I'd be able to follow through with my promise. It was too hard. I questioned what good my visit would do anyway. This was Carter's pattern. I don't think he ever knew the depth of the harm he caused to our marriage. Once he gained his freedom, would he be willing to change how he lived his life and fully recommit to our marriage? I knew what he said but wasn't convinced about what he'd do.

To justify my change of heart, I told myself I was afraid my actions could backfire and become detrimental to his case. In actuality, I was fearful of what my visit would do to me. I didn't want to know anything about that woman or a child they supposedly shared. I didn't think I could handle such an enormous disappointment were the facts contrary to his version of the truth. I couldn't risk it. I just wanted to dwell in the protective confines of my versionary world where I could control the truth I wanted to internalize. I could block out the voices of my friends and family and even myself to uphold the fantasy I'd conditioned myself to believe. It protected my sanity. I didn't want to pick a fight with a stranger that would devastate me if I needed to retreat into the belly of the Trojan Horse he was forcing me to drag into her arena.

Chapter Sixteen

Unforgettable

The radio announcer's voice jumped back into my head and taunted me with new words. *"Grace Mann, the wife of womanizer and abuser Carter Mann, just got the wool pulled over her eyes in dramatic fashion. He convinced her to go on a fool's mission to help him escape prosecution. Fueled by the promises of "I won't cheat on you again" and "That's not my baby", she is going into the situation blindfolded and will have to feel her way through his web of lies. If Grace pulls this off, she gets to continue her journey to happily ever after with a man who beat up his mistress in the morning and went home to celebrate their wedding anniversary that night. Stay tuned to see if Grace makes a complete fool of herself."*

Carter's watch, cell phone, wallet, and wedding ring were in the sealed bag the attorney handed her. The faint sound of the wedding march was playing in my head when I took the ring from the bag and spun it around my index finger. The endless circle of platinum and diamonds sparkled as brightly as it did on our wedding day. Now, everything the ring represented was tarnished by Carter's actions. His version of love included, lying, cheating, abuse, and control, while pretending to honor our marriage. The symbol of his lifetime commitment and devotion became a noose that slipped from his finger and landed around my neck. The longer I stared at it, the harder it was to control my anger. I didn't realize I'd thrown the ring until I heard it clink against the vent. It was responsible for the most brutal assault of my life. He broke something in me that I hadn't been able to piece back together. He still had pieces of me clenched in his hands and fists. I wasn't the same after that night.

I looked around the room and remembered the sights and sounds of one of the worst days of my life. I was so excited about our upcoming vacation. Carter stayed late to clear his schedule for the next two weeks. I'd planned to offer myself up as a pre-vacation treat. Dinner was prepared, the table was set, and soft music was playing. Carter was bringing the wine. I greeted him with kisses and giggles when he walked through the door. When he handed me the bottle of wine, I didn't see his wedding ring. That annoyed me.

"Carter, why aren't you wearing your wedding ring. You know how I feel about that."

"I took it off last night and forgot to put it back on. It's not a big deal."

"It is for me. It's a public symbol of our commitment to each other. It lets everyone know you're married."

"We've been over this before. I don't need to wear that ring to know I'm married."

"You take it off all the time. Maybe I'll stop wearing my wedding ring too."

"With the amount of money I paid for that ring, it'd better be on your finger at all times."

"Since you don't think it matters, maybe I'll conduct my own social experiment. I think I'll act like you. I'm going to run around with no ring, as if I'm not married, and see if any men approach me."

"Don't go there, Grace."

"Why not? Maybe if you always wore your ring, I wouldn't get so many strange phone calls. You're married, but that hasn't stopped you from being with other women."

He looked at me but didn't say a word. I could see the rage building in his eyes. I didn't care. I wanted him to know what I felt when he was unfaithful. I wanted him to feel helpless and unbalanced.

I continued with my rant. I looked directly in his eyes and said, "Well, I want you to know that two can play your game. You've had a head start. Maybe I can catch up with you. It should be easy."

Those words struck a nerve. Immediately, I regretted that last remark. Carter got in my face and through gritted teeth said, "Don't you ever threaten me like that again."

His reaction scared me. I couldn't believe how quickly the argument escalated to an uncomfortable level. I knew it was time to remove myself from the situation. With my eyes still on him, I took one step backward. When I turned to walk away, he grabbed me by my hair and spun me around so quickly, I thought I had whiplash. Before I could think, I was up against the wall with my feet dangling aimlessly beneath me with his hands around my throat. The pressure around my neck caused dizziness from the lack of air. The sound of my pulse drummed away in my ears.

"Carter, I can't breathe. Please let go."

He tightened his grip as my lungs begged for air. I clawed at his hands until his flesh was beneath my fingernails and my knee was in his crotch. Coughing and gasping for air, I ran to the spare bedroom, locked the hallway door, and refilled my lungs after several deep breaths.

He pounded on the door and said, "Unlock the door, Grace."

"Not until you calm down. Leave me alone, Carter, or I'm calling the police." The threat didn't faze him. He wouldn't stop beating on the door. I was scared. I'd just pressed the last digit when Carter entered through the connected bathroom, snatched the receiver from my hand, and hung up the phone. When the police called back, he heard every word as they explained their intent to stop by the house even though it was an accidental call. Carter was furious. He looked at me and said, "You'd better be convincing when they get here. You've got ten minutes."

He spoke like he'd done the drill before. They were knocking at our door in eight minutes. I was all smiles, lies, and apologies. They left without inspecting the house, the skin underneath my scarf, or Carter's hands that were kept deep in his pockets. Carter's demeanor changed as soon as he closed the front door. Calmness was replaced by anger. His spotless public image had been challenged. His reputation was something he valued above everything else. He had to look like he was living his best life, even if it wasn't true. He often told me how hard he fought not to be reminded of the people and things he wanted to forget. The consequences of our actions represented a giant step backward.

Carter's mood was pensive when he turned around. I heard the agitation in his voice when he said, "Grace, what you did tonight was unforgivable. What were you thinking? Were you trying to ruin my reputation? Were you trying to lose all this?"

It appeared Carter didn't want to take ownership of his part of our disagreement. I was willing to claim my role and said, "We both overreacted, and things got out of control. I'm so sorry."

"Of course, you are, Grace. So, what do you think should happen now?"

"Nothing. It's over. We both need to take a deep breath and try to salvage what's left of our Friday night. I don't want this ruining our vacation."

"Over. You think it's over. It's not over for me. I think I need to teach you a lesson."

"What are you talking about? I already said I was sorry. But you can't put your hands on me like that." I sat down on the sofa, removed my scarf, and rubbed my neck. I was certain it was marked. Hopefully, it would be fine by Monday. We had a plane to catch. As for Carter, I would have to give him some extra attention in the bedroom to soothe his bruised ego. I always knew how to make him feel better. We were good at make-up sex.

Carter momentarily left the room. I thought the conversation was over, and he was taking time to let his anger subside. He returned with a gun and a syringe and laid them on the table. My eyes bounced between two objects that normally wouldn't be used at the same time. He laid the gun on the table beside the phone and gently placed his hand on top of mine. When he spoke again, his voice was calm. His words measured. I didn't expect that level of restraint after such an explosive prior verbal exchange.

I couldn't focus on the words coming from his mouth. I was entranced by the shiny death tool on the table. He let me hold it once. That was enough. I didn't like guns and the closeness to death they represented. I never planned to touch it again. But if I had to, I wondered if I could. At that point, I didn't think the union of the three of us would be in my favor. My mind jumped from scenario to scenario. From question to question. From life to one of our deaths. Are there bullets in the gun? I didn't know. Could I get the gun first? I couldn't be sure. Could I muster the courage to shoot him? Maybe. Could I claim self-defense? Probably. Could he really shoot me? Definitely. Was I prepared to die? Not yet.

As if my internal dialogue was being broadcast, he asked, "Do you think you're quick enough to get the gun before I do? Go ahead, Grace. Try. I'll even let you make the first move."

"Why do you have that gun? You know I don't like having a gun in the house."

"But I need it. Just pretend you don't see it. Don't look so worried, Grace, everything will be fine. If anything goes wrong, you can always call the police again."

I looked down at the gun again. A chill ran up my spine. Whatever he'd planned for me involved that revolver. I barely knew anything about guns and didn't know how to

62

tell if it had bullets. I was completely in over my head. He continued to stare at me. His eyes moved from me to the gun several times, taunting me to pick up the weapon. I didn't move. I locked my fingers together, put my hands in my lap, and waited. I was tempted, but not brave.

Chapter Seventeen

Gun Control

When Carter picked up the gun, I knew I was in trouble. I tried to get up from the sofa, but he shoved me back down. The pillows scattered and made room for me. He grabbed me around my neck, tilted my head back, and slowly caressed my face with the tip of the gun. My skin burned along the elongated path. He pulled the gun away from my face, forced my jaws open, and shoved the tip of the barrel into my mouth. My eyes watered when the site scraped the roof of my mouth. He rotated the gun around inside my mouth before he pushed it deeper toward my throat. My gag reflex engaged. I made vomiting sounds as my tongue and throat rejected his gift. He noted my discomfort but was not deterred. He seemed to enjoy the hurt he caused me. It was part of the lesson he wanted to teach. Tears started streaming down my face. I imagined the wildness in his eyes as he whispered in my ear, "Do you think you need to call 911?" I couldn't answer. My mouth was full. All I could do was pray. I was afraid to do anything else. As the tears flowed faster, he licked a few of them from my face before he replaced them with soft kisses. With his mouth resting close to my ear, he whispered, "I hope you know how much I love you, Grace."

My eyes looked wildly around the room in search of a focal point. I just needed something familiar to remind me that I was at my home, with my husband and not with a sadistic stranger. I tasted blood before it mixed with drool, puddled in the floor of my mouth, and dripped down the front of my shirt like water from a leaky faucet. I wanted to swallow what remained but couldn't without resting my lips around the hard exterior of the barrel. I feared any unexpected movement against the gun could prove fatal. I'd never swallowed a bullet before and wondered what it would feel like to die. I prayed I would barely feel the hot lead enter my brain or smell the convergence of gun powder with brain matter. Hopefully, I would die quickly or be too paralyzed to care.

Relief washed over me when he removed the gun from my mouth, and the threat of eating a bullet was alleviated. But what I encountered next was worse, to the point that I prayed for the bullet instead. I was defenseless against the barrage of the lesson he wanted to teach me that night. Several times, I flew across the room like I'd sprouted angel wings. I watched the room fly by like segments of an 8-millimeter film. Each time the floor greeted me, he picked me up and showed me more expressions of his love. When my eyes could focus, I saw scenes in black and white and splashes of distorted color. I saw the look of determination plastered on his face as he intentionally stepped on my left hand. I cried out in pain when he leveraged all of his weight on my ring finger. When he pressed down and moved the ball of his foot back and forth, I felt the ring's diamond cut into my flesh. Then, I heard him say, "I will kill you before I let you embarrass me again."

No one could convince me I wasn't almost there. I was nearly unconscious, but able to whimper, "Please stop, Carter. I've learned my lesson. I'm so sorry. You win. I won't ever do that again. I'm begging you. Please stop."

After I surrendered, so did he. I gave Carter what he wanted. He got his dignity back. The contents of the syringe gave me the relief I wanted. We both were satisfied. Before I passed out, I felt him lift me from the floor and carry me toward our bedroom. I didn't know I was alive until Tuesday. Once I tried to move, I wanted to find the leader of the stampede that trampled over my body. Through the slits of my eyes, I saw Carter laying right beside me. Out of fear, my body stiffened. It relaxed when he picked up my left hand and kissed it. The diamonds on my wedding band glistened on my swollen finger, as did the emerald and diamond bracelet I noticed on my wrist. Undoubtedly, the bracelet was my anniversary gift. I'd have to check the Hallmark anniversary gift list to see what year guns and syringes were recommended. When Carter let go of my hand, I noticed he wasn't wearing his wedding ring. I said nothing. I didn't care if he ever wore it again. After that night, he owned me.

Carter taught me many lessons that day. I learned not to fight back and how good I could beg. I learned I didn't really know the person I'd married and that the gun was fully loaded. When all was said and done, the biggest lesson I learned was that I would never call the police again. Sometimes I question the decisions I made that day. Why hadn't I at least tried to pick up the gun? Not doing so doomed me to everlasting submission. I'd healed but never recovered from the surgical infliction of his dominance. He'd clipped my wings that day. I forgot I knew how to fly.

Chapter Eighteen

Nursery Rhymes

I'd spent the last few days thinking about dark moments in history with my husband. I was surprised by how fresh they felt. Although I didn't dwell on them, I was always conscious of how close I was to that level of retribution. Without the courage to use my voice against him, he trampled on our marriage vows with regularity. Over time, the breaks in my heart became more tolerable. After each betrayal, the jagged edges of pain caused by his infidelity didn't hurt as deeply. I learned to focus on the idea that all those random women were temporary and would vanish as quickly as they appeared. But the stakes were higher this time; there was a child involved. That's where I drew the line. All our other secrets could remain hidden away in the pockets of sadness I kept hidden deep inside. But not a baby. It was permanent. I found that to be morally offensive and potentially expensive. Its presence exposed our dirty laundry. It illegitimated our union and showed the world how trivial the vows of our marriage had become. The baby would be something we couldn't hide.

The morning I drove to the hospital, I was filled with apprehension, curiosity, bravery, hope, and a thousand little anxieties. For different reasons, each one of those fueled me forward. Their intensity multiplied the closer I got to my destination. An overall distrust of my husband silently protested Carter's intervention directive. The pit of my stomach burned with fear of being emotionally ambushed by another lie. My intuition was fighting with my determination. It felt like the music on my car radio was replaced with loud voices telling me to go back home. I begged it for silence. I'd committed to saving our family. I couldn't break my promise; not when I felt so important to my husband. After I parked the car, I took a deep breath and prepared for the unknown.

As I walked into the hospital, I was struck with the irony of my situation. I was entering a place where healing was the goal. I was suffering from an acute case of Angry Wife's Syndrome, something only I could cure. I wondered if meeting Eva would be the prescription I needed. I viewed our pending encounter as my way of settling unrealized scores. Finally, one of the nameless, faceless opportunists' who constantly took jabs at me through the phone, would have an identity. I had no idea how I'd control my anger when I confronted his mistress. I couldn't afford to alienate Eva before I could convince her to drop the charges. The need for her cooperation outweighed my desire to punish an adversary.

Once I stepped inside the elevator, I had the overwhelming desire to stop by the nursery. I wanted to see the baby before confronting the mother. That would give me some indication of the type of woman I was dealing with this time. If the child bore no visible signs of Carter, I would be able to use it as leverage. Lucky for me, there was only one girl in the nursery. As I peered at the baby through the nursery window, conflicting emotions coursed through my body. Maybe she could be Carter's, maybe not. I didn't see anything that couldn't be disputed. Regardless, she was a beautiful gift from God, no matter who her father turned out to be.

I watched the sleeping infant as she wiggled and squirmed out of a nap, exposing the crescent-shaped spot on her hand. I recognized the familial birthmark as the same one that adorned my children, CJ and Taylor. I closed my eyes and prayed the birthmark wouldn't be there when I opened them again. I remembered Carter's pronouncement when our children were born, "I see my family's birthmark. It's proof of our bloodline. That's better than any paternity test I know." His words were prophetic. Carter's DNA fingerprints were still visible on the baby when I opened my eyes. She was his. My husband had fathered a child that wasn't mine.

I stood in solitude surrounded by hospital personnel in a face-to-face confrontation with his unanticipated confession. The effect of that discovery felt like a shock collar had been used on me. The intensity of the current rendered me paralyzed but no longer confused. The explosion of sadness that followed sent the shrapnel of confusion through the layers of lies I'd acted upon. Before I arrived at the hospital, I was scarred but hopeful. That was no longer true. Nothing would ever be the same for me again. I was hurt in a way I didn't know existed. I thought I'd hit rock bottom many times before, but there appeared to be a pit beyond the bottom. I'd just landed there, headfirst. What did his lies mean for me? For my children? For our family?

I shouldn't have been as shocked as I was. I'd expected the outcome to have materialized years earlier. I thought about all the random phone calls at odd hours from strange female voices tethered to the temporary facade he chose. I often imagined who he was when he was with them. In all those moments of speculation, I'd never once imagined he would ever be the man whose heart I was exposed to that day. This dirt was more staining and despotic than I imagined he was capable of. It was on another level. I wondered how someone I knew and loved could hate so deeply and act with such hostility. But why was I surprised? How much different was this act than the ones perpetrated on me for more years than I cared to remember? I wondered if his heart was dead, and the blood that coursed through his veins was black, to match the depths of his soul.

Eva and her baby were forcing me to deal with realities I never wanted to confront. I wanted to hate them and what they represented. I couldn't. I was a mother. I thought about being pregnant with my children. I remembered the expectation, coupled with the uncertainty of healthy births. I couldn't imagine the agony Eva felt when her child was forced to enter the world early because of an assault. The skin around my heart wrenched. Had my hand not felt the increased beating in my chest, I would've thought it'd stopped. My spirit felt the same pain. In the midst of all the ugliness, something beautiful and loving was created. I couldn't take my eyes off her. All wiggly and squirmy and animated, she fought fiercely for each tiny breath exhaled into the universe. That tiny being hit me in the heart and caused it to explode with maternal respect for her mother. She got under my skin. Once I looked into her innocent face, I was so ashamed. I silently apologized to the baby for both our actions then whispered, "Keep fighting baby girl. Keep fighting." No matter the effect her existence would have on my life, I couldn't help but cheer for her, to pray for her. She represented a bright spot in our dark corridor of deceit. How odd. She was so very small for a train.

Chapter Nineteen

Retreat, Retreat

A wave of nausea rippled through my body. My breathing labored; not enough fresh air was filling my lungs. I fought to take the next breath. Sweat dotted my forehead as I tried to recover from the shock of my life. I rested my body against the wall to steady my balance. I had to escape my nightmare inside the sterile confines of the nearest bathroom. The clicking sounds of my heels against the floor annoyed me. They let me know that I was not moving fast enough. I wouldn't be able to outrun the truth I discovered behind the protective barrier of the viewing room. I had been involved in emotional fisticuffs with an infant. It wasn't a fair fight. I had to surrender. She won.

The fervor with which I entered the hospital subsided after my morning meal splashed into the bathroom sink and brought momentary commonality to the porcelain and stainless steel. Although the water restored their separate identities, the smell of my internal revolting lingered. The coolness of the water on my tongue helped as I stood over the sink, trying to regain my composure. I had to rinse my mouth with several handfuls of water to remove the foul taste. I wondered if some of it could be attributed to my impending task. I wet several paper towels and wiped my tongue. I wet several more and placed them on my forehead. I needed to sit down. As much as I hated public bathrooms, when my body relaxed on the toilet seat inside the stall, I felt safe. I just needed a moment to breathe.

My physical reaction to knowing the baby was Carter's surprised me. I had faced many marital adversaries in the past, but none wounded me as much as this one. I kept seeing the birthmark in my mind, contrasted by Carter's vehement paternal denial. I knew it was a possibility; he knew it was all a lie when the words passed through his lips. There was nothing I could do. The spirit of protection for my family dissolved under the flow of tears that ate away at my resolve. Any desire to present myself to the home-wrecker as a symbol of strength abandoned me in the hallway outside the nursery window.

After leaving the stall, I stood in front of the mirror and looked at the person staring back at me. I barely recognized her. Who I saw, I didn't like. I would have to deal with her later. For now, I had to repair my flawed make-up and continue on my mission. Once I used the eye drops to clear the redness, I turned my head from side to side, trying to see if the make-up sufficiently covered my brokenness. I felt I looked good enough to face the woman who was trying to replace my family with her own.

I was still rattled after seeing Carter and Eva's love child. My gut told me to retreat. There was an innocent child fighting for her life and a mother fighting to overcome the trauma of Carter's anger. I muttered to myself, "What are you doing here? Go home. You already know the truth." But I didn't listen. Carter's voice in my head encouraged me to save him. To save us. To save our family. Sadly, I'd made him a promise I would have to keep, no matter how much my brain and my soul protested.

For my own selfish reasons, I had to see her; to look in the eyes of one of the women who forced me into reality. Seeing one of the pillars that made up the wall that separated me from my happily ever after was long overdue. I had to try to fight for my children and my current lifestyle. I didn't know what we would do without their father and the financial support he provided. I reasoned that we deserved to remain in comfortable surroundings. If the topic came up, I wouldn't object if she wanted him to pay child support. I paused and thought about the solution I'd just considered. With all that was going on, my overriding concern was about money and status. At that moment, I felt street puddle shallow.

Chapter Twenty

The Good Soldier

My mind traveled over the task given to me by my husband. When I first entered the hospital, I was prepared to go to battle with the lying hussie who was trying to take away my family. But I lost my desire at the nursery window. I scolded myself for not aborting the meeting once I recognized the familial DNA stamp on the baby. I had been betrayed once again. With the new information I'd gathered, my assignment had become mission impossible. But like a good soldier, something inside urged me to see it through to the end. The closer I got to his mistress's room, the heavier my feet felt. I whispered desperate prayers for the strength to get me through my assignment. 'Please, God, don't let me cry again in front of her. I can't expose my weakness to my mortal enemy. I have to be strong. Don't let me be weak again today."

I stood at the door momentarily before I found the courage to cross its threshold. Part of me wanted to turn around and run, not walk, back to the safety of my illusions, and the comfort of the version of truth I created for myself. It was wandering the halls of the hospital looking for me. I had to abandon it there; it couldn't go back home with me. Eventually, it would find its way to the morgue of truth. But it wouldn't be lonely. I was certain several other misconceptions would join it once I completed my wifely duties of persuasion.

No matter how long I waited, I would never be ready for the meeting. I wanted to be anywhere but there. I was still reeling from my visit to the nursery. I had not yet calmed down from the onslaught of emotions I'd experienced while looking at the fight for survival being exhibited by the tiny miracle of life. I couldn't outrun the knowledge that the baby would forever be bonded to my existence through my husband and my children.

I knocked and was granted permission to enter by a gentle, female voice on the other side of the door. I didn't know what to expect once I accepted the invitation. I wasn't sure how she would respond to me once she figured out the enemy had invaded her territory. The person whose face I saw didn't resemble the one I'd conjured up in my mind. When our eyes met, I understood how Carter could have been enamored with her. Even behind the bruises and swelling, she was stunning. Eva was definitely his type. She reminded me so much of a younger version of myself. I could see how Carter had been drawn to her. Without the prominent bruising, we could've passed for sisters. But unlike me, I saw a level of strength and courage I lacked. I wanted to applaud her for standing up for herself. I remembered how my hand trembled as it hovered over the phone after one of Carter's attacks. I was too hurt to ignore the need for medical attention but too afraid to publicly acknowledge his physical impropriety. I'd made that phone call once and was subjected to the most vicious beating of my marital existence. My mind refocused and I understood the brutality that culminated in the remnants of painted objections on her face. But one phone call had saved Eva's life and the life of her child. Maybe I should've made call number two.

Chapter Twenty-One

Puppets

History always repeats itself. Sometimes it even looks different. But not this time. When I looked at Eva and the condition of her battered face, I winced. It was the same as my portrait of Carter's anger landscape. I easily recognized the byproducts of his hands. I'd worn those same familiar color palettes more times than I'd ever admit. There was no need to ask what happened; I knew. He got angry. And from the looks of things, he was really mad. I couldn't see the depth of bruising hidden behind those inefficient hospital garments and was glad to be shielded from the entire aftermath of his ugliness. I already knew what that looked like. It was something else we shared besides being the mother of his children.

I didn't believe I could convince Eva that Carter was worth saving. She already knew he wasn't. In some ways, so did I. It took everything in me not to expose my disbelief in the required outcome of my husband's intentions of our meeting. I hoped my eyes would not betray the secret mission I had concealed in my heart. My eyes had to appear focused and not dart wildly around the room, as they often did when I was nervous. I hoped my makeup wouldn't show any hints of my recent battle with composure at the nursery window. I had to keep telling myself that my family was at stake, and I was the only one who could save it now.

I spoke first. "Hello, Eva. I'm Grace. Carter's wife."

She remained silent as the words sunk in. I could tell my presence was unexpected. Shocking would be a better word. She cocked her head slightly and returned my gaze. I had to look away. My eyes found the tranquility of the blue sky that landscaped the freedom that beckoned me beyond the window. If the window were open, I believe I could have jumped. It would've been the easy way out of this impossible mission. She offered me the chair beside her bed. I quickly sat down. My legs were getting weak.

While sitting on the bed, she looked me in the eyes and said, "Forgive me, but until recently, I thought his name was Ben Wilson. Hearing him being called by another name will take some getting used to."

"I see." Our common confusion was paralyzing, and I internally repeated my husband's pseudonym, trying to find words to overcome the shock. I found none.

"I think I know why you're here."

"Do you?"

'Yes. This is about your husband, the father of my child."

My shame multiplied. I shook my head in affirmation.

"First, let me say that I owe you an apology. You have every right to be upset with me. I'm so ashamed."

Eva dropped her head and momentarily stared at the floor. I was shocked by her demonstration of humility. I didn't expect our conversation to begin with an apology from his other woman. It was atypical for a mistress.

"Grace, I didn't know he was married. I would never willingly become involved with a married man. My parents raised me better than that. He never wore a wedding ring. I often studied his hand, looking for some indicator. I never saw anything; no tan line, no indentation, nothing."

I raised my eyebrow after hearing the revelation within her confession. As much as I didn't want to trust her, that part sounded true. We'd argued many times about the missing ring. Maybe it was my own history that caused me to question her motives for becoming involved with my husband. My past sins knocked on my heart and stroked my ego with the broad brush of *"I know you don't believe that."* No way she didn't know he was married when they met. No way she could be that innocent.

I asked her, "When did you find out?"

"I overheard him talking to your child the night before your anniversary. I can't remember the words verbatim, but he promised he hadn't forgotten and to put mommy on the phone. That's all I heard before I crept back into the bathroom. I slept on the couch that night. The next day I confronted him. I can't remember much else until I woke up here. I thought my baby was dead. It was a miracle we survived."

I couldn't sit in that chair any longer. I had to release some of the nervous tension that continued to pile up in my body. It felt like bricks were sitting on my shoulders. I stood up and walked over to the window. I was glad my back was to her. She wouldn't be able to see the turmoil in my eyes.

"Oh God," I thought. "I overheard that conversation between my husband and Taylor." That revelation made me sick to my stomach again. Although I thought my prior visit to the bathroom released all my breakfast, I threw up in my mouth a little bit when the timing significance of Carter's attack became apparent. I cleared my throat of the seepage but had no choice but to swallow. I didn't know how cows did it. Maybe it was a preview of the bitter taste from words I would have to eat later.

I moved away from the window and stood by the chair. I swallowed hard and completed my mission. My vocal cords burned as I begged for the freedom of her abuser. The desperation that rolled from my lips was in my voice but with Carter's words. The lying, cheating, manipulative snake was now a ventriloquist and I was his dummy. I shifted my body to ensure the threads and strings he was pulling were not visible. I knew what I was doing was wrong. I regretted every word and every action I had taken on Carter's behalf that day. But what choice did I have? I couldn't be like Carter. I didn't want to break my promise.

I pleaded with my tears to stay put. They ignored me. I wiped them away as quickly as possible before trying to speak again. "Please Eva," was all I could say before my mind and body betrayed me. Uncontrollable tears flowed from my eyes, causing Eva to hug me in my distress. I was surprised but grateful for the unexpected shoulder to cry on. She joined me in the release of pent-up sorrow. I was bonding with another heiress of Carter's abuse. We were mutually saddened by his actions, but our focus was in different directions. I was sure we weren't crying for the same reason. Maybe some of her tears were for me.

When we regained our composure, she said, "I'm sorry, Grace. I can't give you what he wants. It's out of my hands and never should've been in yours. None of this is your fault. Don't share his blame. Ben left me and my child to die in that apartment and he, alone, will have to pay for what he did. He'll have to stand trial."

I wasn't surprised by her response. I couldn't imagine how she felt. Neither could she imagine my pain. I apologized for my intrusion and thanked her for listening. Once I'd made it to the door, Eva called my name. When I turned around, she searched my eyes and said, "How many times has your face looked like mine?"

Carter had branded me with his abuse, and Eva quickly recognized it. I couldn't think of a believable response before I exited the room. The puppet show was over.

Chapter Twenty-Two

Rattled

Eva's parting question lingered in my ears as the door to her room closed behind me. Even if I tried, I couldn't keep those words from burrowing further into my soul. She saw me. My make-up couldn't cover up my fear and brokenness. She saw who I tried so hard to hide from the world. I practically ran to the elevator, trying to get as far away from that room as quickly as possible. As I waited for the elevator, I felt her haunting embrace. I got goosebumps.

Once inside the elevator, the walls began to close in on me. I paced inside the small confined space like a caged animal. It was hard to take a deep breath. I needed fresh air. Although I pushed the lobby button several times in rapid succession, the elevator car was not moving fast enough. There was nowhere to run. I was trapped. I steadied myself with the rail and pleaded with my body to support the extra weight I now carried. I felt at any moment I'd trip the over-weight capacity sensors and get stuck between two floors. That would only add to my nightmare. When the elevator doors finally opened, I walked briskly from the hospital, being ushered by recent words and deeds I couldn't be proud of.

The fresh air I sought while inside the hospital never materialized. The outside air was dense and thick. It clung to my lungs but added no relief from my suffering. I was sweating profusely by the time I got into my vehicle and turned the car's air conditioner on full blast. It couldn't blow air quickly enough to cool down the furnace of shame I'd just stoked by my encounter with my husband's victims. It felt like the heater was on, and I was wrapped in a wool blanket. As quickly as I'd closed the car door, I opened it again, leaned over the threshold, and threw up. The matted strings of hair plastered against my forehead didn't move. I gently wiped my mouth and settled into my safe surroundings.

As soon as I closed the car door, I completely fell apart. I gripped the steering wheel with both hands and began to pound my head against it in rapid succession. I wanted to replace one form of pain with another until the physical pain extinguished my mental anguish. I needed to escape the dark disappointments I'd just orchestrated. I screamed and cried inside my BMW decompression chamber until my nausea subsided, the shrill sounds escaping from my throat quieted down, and the next batch of tears was released. But after all that, total relief evaded me. All my steering wheel massage produced was a bruised forehead and a splitting headache. I didn't care. I deserved it all.

The ride home was so different from the ride to the hospital. Driving away from the building didn't mean I could escape the problems my visit unearthed. As I watched the building grow smaller, I knew the problems I drove home with would undoubtedly grow larger and larger. Once again, I'd been exploited by my husband.

Chapter Twenty-Three

After Action Report

Pulling into my driveway gave me a sense of relief. I was happy to finally be home. I remembered leaving the hospital but was oblivious to the sights and sounds the trip possessed. I was not the same person I was when I left that morning. Everything in my world shifted after that elevator ride. My thoughts were still at the hospital with Eva and her baby. I needed something to take my mind off them and every troubling aspect of my visit. Alcohol and a hot bath were my escape.

I submerged every part of my body into the water up to my neck. The fragrant steam filled my nostrils and gave me a few moments of temporary relaxation. Elevated thought patterns returned to the hospital disaster I was trying so hard to forget. Feelings of devastation surrounded me. I had nowhere to run. I didn't know how to escape those feelings. I thought about banging my head against the side of the tub until I was unconscious before the lungs of my lifeless body filled with water. It would look like an unfortunate accident brought about by too much alcohol and a slippery surface. But I loved my children too much to add more uncertainty to their lives.

Despite the suicidal thoughts I'd entertained, the bath, along with two more glasses of wine, relaxed me. My mind was blank for a few minutes before the events of that day intruded into my quiet place. I couldn't help but replay the low points of the day. They became the only thing I could think about. I'd trespassed on his victims' lives to protect my position and got more than I'd bargained for. I couldn't store away the opened gifts of deceit received from my husband's continued lack of honesty. What a fool I continued to be for Carter's affection. He'd devised a grand plan for his freedom and didn't care who got hurt in its execution. As always, he never considered anyone but himself. I was suckered into a fool's rendezvous and got humiliated again. Now I was dealing with the knowledge of the baby whose existence he denied. I was confident he knew it was his child the entire time. Eva was too emotionally involved with him for it to be anyone else's. I didn't know her well, but something about her seemed genuine.

Today, I saw the face of love, and it affected me more than I wanted to admit. It wasn't in the portrait of the man I married whose face proudly hung over the fireplace. It was in the face of the woman who fought for her baby and could now celebrate with her. The love and determination she showed for her child, in the midst of her terror, was unimaginable. I could learn something from her example. It was evident that beyond the bruises was an internal reservoir, full of strength and character, that would become stronger and more saturated with love, as the afterbirth of the traumatic experience subsided.

The ripple effect of his desperate actions continued to expand. I stared down into the wine glass and became envious of the dark liquid. Its world consisted of the confined spaces of a glass perimeter. How I wished my current world had such defined boundaries. My world had an uncontained debris field wider than I could get my thoughts around. It would continue to be discovered generations after I took my last breath. Our children and the next generation of children would have to cope with the actions of parents whose selfishness cast shadows over their entire lives. Out of nowhere, Carter's face pierced the dark recesses of my mind. I took a big gulp of the wine and swallowed hard. As much as I didn't want to think about him, there he was, sitting inside that coffee shop, hiding a monster behind that perfect smile. I was one cup of coffee away from a different life.

Chapter Twenty-Four

Baby Steps

The hot bath, but mostly the wine, worked its magic so well that I slept on top of the covers in my bathrobe. The alcohol-induced sleep was what my body needed. I could've done without the pounding headache and the fuzzy mind. The first sip of badly needed black coffee was bitter. I had a hard time getting it down. It tasted like it was laced with regret, pity, and sorrow. It reminded me of my life with Carter. Before we married, I was different. Dreams of following in the footsteps of my mother, a nurse, and my grandmother, a midwife, got lost once he took over my life. There was something about caring for others that made me happy. I'd been caring for dolls and teddy bears for as long as I could remember. I listened to their heartbeat with headphones, gave shots with ink pens, looked in ears with a magnifying glass, and wasted boxes of tissue and scotch tape creating bandages. I wondered if I should long for that dream again. Maybe when everything was over, I'd revisit that dream.

The mental clarity I sought from the coffee turned out to be a double-edged sword. The pounding stopped but my mind awakened. More thoughts of yesterday raced forward. I was still being hunted by the sights and sounds of the hospital. I wondered how I would've felt had I not gone to the nursery. I heard the voice of my mother say, "When you go looking for something, don't be surprised when you find it."

Lesson learned. I rationalized that the results of the paternity test were pending, and the findings would be revealed through the court documents. At least I had an early warning.

Acting on selfish motives, I got more from the visit than I'd intended and nothing I'd expected. Not only was I shocked by seeing Carter's baby but also by the actions of her mother. The inherent kindness Eva showed stuck with me well beyond our initial embrace. Even after she'd known my true identity, she didn't go into attack mode. Her first instinct was to apologize. I hadn't expected that from the woman Carter described. She held the ultimate wild card that would remain valid for eighteen years, but I didn't detect an opportunistic aura. Missing from her eyes were the hints of a successful campaign coming to fruition. Instead, I saw honesty and regret. That baffled me. If I were in her shoes, I would've had a plan in place after the first positive pregnancy test.

There was something about Eva's character I knew would stay with me long after I settled back into my uncomfortable, comfort zone. Logic, championed by bitterness, dictated I should hate Eva, but something deeper inside sought a show of compassion. Maybe it was because I'd met another heiress of Carter's abuse. Our coronation ceremony included a crown of lumps and bruises, consecrated by a scepter filled with his twisted form of love. I wasn't sure, but perhaps some of my bitterness toward her was the byproduct of years spent marinating in the juices of a bad marriage. I was awed by her example of a gentle spirit filled with a strength I didn't know existed. Seeing the fight in her freed something in me I'd imprisoned long ago.

I thought about my life and the constant backing away from myself I'd experienced once I was under Carter's control. I'd lost my identity. I wondered which closet or jewelry box contained my backbone. My common sense had been parked in the three-car garage and abandoned; my hopes and dreams traded for line items on an American Express billing statement. I kept charging against my freedom month after month, year after year, tear after tear, bruise after bruise, scar after scar. Because I feared my bill would never be paid in full, I felt like an indentured servant. I thought about the actions Eva took against my husband and was moved by her convictions and bravery. If some of her rubbed off on me during our embrace, maybe one day I'd be able to fly again.

My thoughts turned from Eva to the baby. The child had to be more important than the bruised bodies and egos of her mother and me. She lay isolated and shielded from the turmoil that hovered around her existence. Even the gentlest encounter had the potential to impact their beautiful creation. Her only job was to breathe and remain oblivious to the mess that had been created by her father. Her father. How peculiar that I spoke of him as if I didn't know him, even though he was my husband. He wouldn't be able to deny this living truth.

Chapter Twenty-Five

Introductions

Another night's struggle with unpeaceful memories had me wrapped in its cloak of pain. The longer I laid there, the easier it became for the mental uprising to continue. The moment my eyes opened, my first thoughts were of Eva's baby. The tiny being had more of an effect on me than I thought was possible for someone whose existence I had every right to despise. I just found out about her less than a week ago in the most egregious manner. Somehow, none of that seemed to matter. That baby changed me. She stuck to me like the residual dust that gets left behind on fingers that touched the fragile wings of a butterfly.

Compassion and concern double-teamed me, and like manna from heaven, drenched my mind with emotions I couldn't define but felt so strongly. I recalled what it was like to lose a child. The fear, the loneliness, and the shame of complacency still haunted me. I didn't fight back. Eva and her baby did. Maybe I could absorb some of their courage by peering through the sterile viewing window.

Before I had time to object, I was in my car, headed in the direction of the hospital. My last journey there ended in nauseated shrills of defeat and shame. I thought after I rescued my husband from the lies of a scorned woman, he would love me again. Instead, his lies got louder, and I got weaker. I should've recused myself from that impossible mission. Everything I thought I would gain, I lost. But with the confirmation of the betrayal, my mindset shifted. Something intriguing about that mother and daughter gnawed at my soul and forced me to want to know more and care more about them from a place of respect. I respected Eva's sincerity and her apology as she opened up to me about her inexperienced assessment of my husband's lack of marital integrity. She graced me with more than I expected or thought I was entitled to. That took a level of character and strength I no longer possessed. Mine had been buried under a heap of lies and make-up. I was happy that no one looked behind the curtain that shielded my false face, the same face Eva saw right through.

I stood at the observation window, transfixed on my husband's baby. There was something about her that kept drawing me in each time I gazed upon her face. I couldn't look away from one of my perceived enemies who stood between me and my happily sordid after. I mentally compared her features to those of my children. The only physical attribute of note was the unmistakable birthmark. How peaceful she looked. What a struggle it must have been to survive the brutal arrogance of Ben's attack. I hated Ben. I didn't know him but was familiar with the evil it took to attack a pregnant woman. I knew Carter. He and Ben were twins.

I was lost in thought and didn't notice the two other people who joined me. I was startled when I turned around and saw Eva, along with the woman from the arraignment. Their similar features led me to believe they were mother and daughter. The older woman's quizzical scowl was in stark contrast to Eva's smiling eyes. Had I been in Eva's mother's shoes, my reaction would probably have been the same. I would've wondered what motive lurked behind the eyes of a distrustful spouse. Was there harm awaiting my offspring's seed? Could there possibly be any genuine concern about something that would continually be a reminder of infidelity and lies? Was I somehow plotting to destroy the secret I couldn't hide? But I had no hidden motive—just motherly concern.

Eva's mother stepped protectively between her daughter and me and asked, "What the hell are you doing here?"

Her eyes latched on to my face and wouldn't let go as she awaited my response. I don't think she blinked once as I searched for an answer that would somehow cause her eyes to detach from my face. My throat closed off any sound that might eek from my vocal cords. All I could do was look off into the distance.

Although I didn't expect those words, I understood the nature of her concern. I was speechless and a bit startled. It showed on my face. Eva's quiet peacemaker demeanor took control of the direction of the conversation. She calmly placed her hand on her mother's shoulder and said, "It's fine, mama. It's okay. This is Ben's, excuse me, Carter's wife, Grace. We met the other day."

"I know who she is. I've seen her at that big, gated house they live in up on that hill."

Her response caught me by surprise. How did she know where I lived? Maybe I should be more fearful of her than I pretended not to be. I instinctively thought about the safety of my children. Then it clicked. I fully understood Eva's mother's rapid transition into protect mode. It was justified.

"I still want to know why she's here. I'm sure he probably sent her."

I thought to myself, "Not this time." I hoped my shame didn't show on my face. I deserved her resentment for invading Eva's healing place with my fated mission to save my family. Inevitably, I'd failed. But who was I kidding? It had been too late to salvage our family unit a long time ago.

Eva took her mother by her shoulders and turned her around. When they were face-to-face, I deeply exhaled and released some of the tension in my body. I was melting under her mother's constant gaze.

Eva's depth of character continued to astound me when she said, "Grace didn't do anything to me. Please try to understand that she is not responsible for Ben's actions."

Ben. She said, Ben. Even though I didn't know him, I hated Ben. I wanted to think that only Ben, not Carter, could exhibit such brutality toward a pregnant woman. I couldn't. I would be lying if I thought otherwise. I'd often felt the expression of his love against my face during all of my pregnancies.

"I'm just as responsible for this mess as her husband. I harmed Grace. So, we can't punish her. It's not fair."

"Fair? Let's talk about what's fair. Was it fair when that man lied to you, beat you, and left you and your baby for dead?" Eva's mother didn't wait for a response. She answered her own question. "No! So please don't talk to me about what's fair. None of this is fair to you. Not from Ben and certainly not from her, who's standing there looking at you and my grandbaby. She needs to know that I don't play when it comes to protecting you. She needs to know how angry I am."

"I think she knows, Mama."

"She's lucky that philandering husband of hers is still in one piece. I just couldn't get to him before the police did." She dropped her head toward the floor, then looked up again with tears in her eyes. There was a pause before she cleared her throat, regained her composure, and finally said, "I was here, at this hospital, with you, praying after that coward beat you within an inch of your life. And, he nearly took the life of your child. His own child. How do you think I'm supposed to feel? No parent is worthy of the air they breathe if they don't do everything within their power to protect their children. He has to pay for this."

Although the anger in her voice was meant for my husband, its impact landed squarely on me. I began to understand the emotional devastation of his brutal attack against an innocent mother and child. Before now, the hypothetical impact of his brutality was only conjecture. In that brief moment, I became an eyewitness to his collateral damage.

Eva calmly replied, "Mama, save your anger for the right person. Grace is not that person. We both are victims. I'm not blameless either."

I saw the sincerity in her eyes as she pleaded with her mother for perspective. Her maturity level illustrated how much depth I lacked.

Grace continued her pleas. "Big Mama once told me that the longer you hold on to hurt, the deeper it burrows into your soul. I'm gonna get through this. I have to. Joy needs me. Not just the broken me with missing pieces. All of me. And, we both are gonna need you."

Eva's mother let those words sink in for a moment. Her expression changed when she chuckled and said, "Don't make me wish I still had my knife."

Although she laughed, that threat was directed at me and I whole-heartedly believed in the veracity of her words. I continued to awkwardly stand there, wishing I could have completed my adjusted assignment undetected. But with the frequency of my visits to check on the baby, the odds against not being discovered dwindled. This encounter was my destiny.

When Eva's mother turned around, her face and eyes continued to express her displeasure with my presence. She kept her guard up, although she managed to relax the lines in her furrowed brow. Her body never moved too far away from her daughter. What an awkward triangle of truth we made. Each of us approached the situation from different angles, with different motives. Eva moved around from behind her mother and stood next to me. As we looked together through the viewing window, she said, "Grace, meet Joy."

I'd been properly introduced to my children's sister. How would I break the news to my family when I had so much trouble accepting it myself?

Chapter Twenty-Six

Disrespected

I was dreading the visit with Carter. I knew he didn't want to see me as much as he wanted to know if I'd convinced Eva not to move forward with her case. I tried to prepare myself mentally for his reaction.

When I put the phone up to my ear, he never asked about the kids or how I was doing. His first question was, "Did you talk to Eva?"

I was quite annoyed when I responded, "Yes, I did."

"And?"

"She won't do it."

He didn't like my response. I could see the anger in his eyes. Even with the glass between us, I was still afraid of Carter. Moments of terror flashed through my mind as I remembered how he expelled that rage. I braced myself for the unknown. He stared at me momentarily before he responded, "I asked you to do one simple thing, and you can't even do that. What good are you?"

I cringed at his outburst. Even behind bars, he remained arrogant. He'd enjoyed himself to the fullest, and when his escapades exceeded his common sense, I was asked to sacrifice my dignity to save him. His angry tone continued as he held up his index finger and said, "One thing, Grace. I asked you to do one simple thing! You couldn't even do that!"

I began to shrink into my seat and meekly said, "I tried, Carter. I don't think you realize how badly she was hurt. Maybe she just needs a little more time."

"I've given you enough time to persuade her. We can't let this go to trial. My reputation will be ruined."

His eyes became wilder as he pounded his fist on the counter and asked, "What does she want from me? Does she want me to beg? I'm not willing to give her that satisfaction."

I didn't have time to respond before Carter spoke again. His anger toward me continued, "After all I've done for you, I can't believe how useless you've been to me. If I don't get out of here, it's all your fault!"

I couldn't believe my ears. I was being blamed for his still being in jail. What more did he expect me to do? He'd been less than forthright. I wasn't prepared to speak to the mother of his child. I went there assured of the impossibility of his paternity. At a time when I needed him to just be honest with me, he chose to continue to try to hide behind the lies. It felt like he spat in my face, cleaned the spittle, and spat in my face again. He didn't understand the blow to my dignity that I sustained begging for his freedom. All he could think about was himself. What about me and how I felt? As usual, my feelings were overlooked.

I couldn't control my irritation when I asked, "What about the baby?"

"What about it?"

"She's yours. I'm sure of it."

"What are you talking about? How many times do I have to say it? That is not my baby. When are you gonna get that through your head?"

"She has your family's birthmark, Carter. It's the same one that's on our children."

"No way. No way!" he said as he shook his head in disbelief.

Before I went to the hospital, I'd been willfully confused by the baby issue, based on my belief in my husband. Now we both knew the truth. He'd admitted the affair but denied the baby. But every sin knows its sinner, and every secret finds its way to the light. I needed my sunglasses to block the glare.

I was beginning to entertain thoughts of hatred toward my husband. Never had I ever been in that mindset before. I sat with the phone in my hand and focused on the sound of blood rushing in my ear. It matched my heartbeat. I couldn't contain the urge to lash out at him in anger as the sound got louder and louder. Over the years, my bravery developed laryngitis. Today it found its voice. I had nothing more to lose. My thoughts exploded into the air. "You don't get to blame me for any of this mess, Carter. You did this all by yourself! You had an affair! You beat that woman to a bloody pulp and tried to kill that baby! Your own baby! Now, you have the nerve to sit in jail and treat me like I'm in there, and you're out here. How dare you!"

When I stood up, something about him changed. He apologized and begged me to sit back down. I was sure his apology was not out of a sense of remorse for his harsh words. It was another way for him to control me.

I remained standing. I'd had enough for that day. Before I walked away, I said, "No matter how you look at it, the truth will always be the truth. It will never change. Neither will you! Call the guard. It's time for you to go back to your cell. I'm going home." I paused for a moment then said, "By the way, Carter, your child's name is Joy. And in case you're interested, both Eva and your baby are going to be fine." Then I slammed down the phone and walked away. Once again, everyone was looking.

Chapter Twenty-Seven

Matters of the Heart

I was angry as I drove home after my visit with Carter. It was hard getting over the fact that he belittled me in front of everybody who gathered in a place where time was limited, broken plans were readjusted, and promises of repentance filled the air. I'd conditioned him to think that whatever he required from me, he got. What he wanted this time was out of my control. Any progress I thought we'd make with our marriage evaporated. Once again, I'd stuck my neck out for Carter, and it got chopped off.

From the beginning, I believed in my husband. I was so full of life in the early stages of our marriage. No one could tell me the depths of our union had a bottom. It was what I'd been conditioned to do and how I'd been conditioned to think. I loved him from the bottom, to the top and from all sides of my heart. Regretfully, my heart often worked against me. It cluttered my mind, distorted my vision, and at times, rendered me helpless. Yet, I kept putting it in charge. I served my heart up to my husband on a platter; he ate all of it, then walked away. I never imagined my heart needed to be protected from my husband. Clearly, I didn't know the person I pledged my life to until we both died. As I watched our marriage dissolve into a plate of crumbs, I was forced to accept what I denied in my spirit. One-sided love would never be enough.

The heart is often stretched beyond its limits while dealing with emotional and physical expectations. It can travel without leaving our bodies and allows us to share it with others, while it still pumps blood for our existence. We give it away, hoping it doesn't return to us shattered in pieces that can't be reassembled. It can be our secret weapon and our most formidable foe. After being broken, it can rejuvenate itself and open up again to the possibility of being regifted. I'd known all sides of the journey. Once I gave it to Carter, my heart attacked me.

It took years to realize that my heart wanted what it wanted but seldom knew what it needed. Who I chose to love was up to me. Despite our jaded history, I chose to continue to love my husband and him only. His re-offense rate was high, yet I kept putting my heart on the line. That was all I knew to do when the thought of what could be took charge. I found ways to survive the emotional spasms of the relationship, hoping it led me to the type of love I desired. In those moments, I should've put a restraining order on my heart to keep it away from my husband. It kept wanting to have empathy for him, even after years of being broken and knocked around by his angry love. At times, it persuaded me to lose connection with the things and the other people in my life that loved me first. My heart and my mind were constantly in conflict. No matter which won, I would lose.

Carter and I loved differently. I loved deeply; I didn't believe he loved at all. He constantly broke my heart. Even while broken, it still had to sustain my human existence while my spirit and soul withered away in defeat. Losing the sanctity of our marriage felt like hell was attacking me in my most vulnerable region. Over time, my heart got smaller, an unfortunate side effect of years of neglect. The broken parts of it were scattered over years of disappointment and regret. Fragments of it were planted in the soil of sadness and watered by infidelity and disruption.

Who was Carter Mann? I'd been married to him for years but couldn't answer that question. A ghostwriter penned the group of lies he publicly masqueraded as himself. I often wondered how he managed multiple personas with just one body. Surely there wasn't enough space for either to be comfortable because of the constant fight for dominance. I saw a decent person one minute, a monster hidden behind a cloak of smiles the next. I never knew who he would become in the blink of an eye. I wouldn't be surprised if he got confused about which one was on display. In some respects, I think the mental contradictions made him fragile. At times, it felt as if he was wrestling with a league of demons who exited his body through pores of aggression. Other times, when his guard was down, I saw sound bites of a person whose heart I longed to merge with my own.

Where Carter hid his love remained a mystery. He kept that portion of himself hidden from me and the world. For years, I'd been on a scavenger hunt, with limited clues, trying to find it. He never opened up and let me into his heart. That passageway to his soul was too constricted for love to flow freely. I felt sorry for him. The inherent sounds of love, that echo within all beings, were muffled inside his core. Something severed that connection. Maybe if he ever showed a hint of compassion, the pre-broken person would have a chance to thrive. I could only imagine what our marriage would look like if he ever had the courage to try.

Chapter Twenty-Eight

Conflict Resolution

In my quest for marital significance, I abandoned myself and my needs when I only concentrated on his. My mindset about myself changed after I surrendered everything to my husband. Wasn't that what I was supposed to do? The preacher said, and I committed to our becoming one. How could I be a separate person and still honor the essence of my vows? And after everything it took to coax Carter away from his former fiancé, I had to be everything he wanted me to be. Seeds I had sewn years earlier became ripe for harvest. I didn't have the guts to complain. I knew I was owed.

From the moment we met, I wanted to pretend his past never existed. It never mattered that he had a fiancé when he met me. Even when I learned of her existence, I was happy to move forward with the relationship. He was relentless in his pursuit of me. I didn't object. Technically, I wasn't cheating, he was. Besides, neither of us were married. But now we were, and there were other women. I'd fought hard for the man I married and wasn't prepared to make it easy for those lined up to displace me. I knew how his previous fiancé felt times ten. Because of my shameful actions, I figured my marital upheaval was just desserts for the tactics I deployed to corral a husband.

People reveal themselves over time. I didn't like what my husband revealed. Carter's dirty footprints of desire continued to trample across the fabric of our lives. I believed the part in our vows about forsaking all others. Apparently, he was distracted during that part of the ceremony. It took about two years after the bug incident for him to show signs of extramarital activity again. Although I'd strongly recommended counseling after his first affair, he felt we didn't need outsiders telling us what would be best for our marriage. He thought we were best suited for that task. I understood his response but didn't agree. Our vows were as fragile as tissue paper.

We needed help, but my ego whispered to me that I could make him better. He promised he would change, so I had hope. Deep inside, I knew it was a longshot. It didn't take long for my hypersensitive infidelity barometer to forecast a change. I could feel when the cheating started again, even though he continued the pretense of being fully vested in our marriage. I continued to get physical love, time, gifts, and kisses, but I could detect something was different. Our bond was being disrupted. My body signaled an alert that another woman had entered our world. The thing I feared the most happened again and I was powerless to stop it. I found myself in the middle of another competition for my husband that I didn't enter. I was losing. My role as a wife, his port of call for intimacy had been outsourced.

When we were together, I allowed my intuition to reign, even though all outward signs of marital trespass remained concealed. I waited for a slip of the tongue to provide tangible evidence of deception. I thought I'd be able to hear conjecture in his voice or detect slight nuances in his mannerisms and patterns. But there was nothing. The same hidden agenda remained concealed behind his mask. He didn't know how to be anyone except who he was. I saw that years ago, but I held out hope that my commitment and support would soothe the ravenous beast in his soul long enough for decency to find a place to root. That never happened. His garden was too full of rocks, and the seeds of contentment I sought to plant couldn't be cultivated in such untilled, hard-packed soil. The tears, blood, and mucous that flowed from my body failed to irrigate his soul. They passed through his being like water through a sieve. No traces of my anguish made much of a lasting impact. They were but a momentary distraction that only lasted as long as it took for him to become restless. Then, the insults and the fights would come. It was his way of justifying the distance between us as he sought companionship with another woman.

Victim or fool. I remember asking that of a gentle voice on the other end of the phone line, which one she turned out to be. I had no sympathy. I asked myself the same question. I was afraid to hear the answer. It was hard to tell if I'd been a victim or a fool. At times, I'd been both. I couldn't decide which was worse. I was a victim of his lies, his disease, his control, his fists, and my heart's deepest desire. Like a fool, I'd protected him, lied to my family about him, refused to hold him accountable for his actions, forgave him, and let him back into my heart. Just like all the other women who were lured in by his lies, I had a choice. I decided to remain the fool. I didn't want to challenge anything. I wanted to exist in factual limbo for as long as it shielded me from the truth.

The destruction caused by Carter's actions was never felt by him. He was an agent of deceit, sowing seeds of discourse and corruption through our marriage. When he got caught, it didn't faze him. He continued, even after his actions were uncovered. The more he strayed, the bolder the other women became. Their methods were as calculated and precise as Mike Tyson but as unpredictable as Buster Douglas. At any time, they would pop up like a jack-in-the-box with startling faces, infinite smiles, and disheartening details.

Their job was to let you know they were there. It didn't matter if they were hidden or in plain sight. They were the spoilers and were good at their job. They wanted you to know that at some point your trust had been undermined by your mate's excursions into adultery. They were responsible for the constant uneasiness that leaked into every thought and quiet moment when you were apart. They wanted you always wondering and running inquisitive, anxious fingers over the keypad after each call from strange numbers. It was all part of a game I was forced into because of my husband. I often quieted my conscience with justifications that were superficial and unworthy of being related to such weighty circumstances. All these tricks were in the man-stealing play-book I'd become acquainted with while being married. It was my job to monitor our progress and make adjustments to get us back on track.

As Carter's infidelity got worse, he held our vows at arm's length. I had to be on stilts to reach the apex of his lies and deceit. Each time a business trip lasted longer than anticipated, I wondered what her name was. I often went scent-searching on his clothes as I gathered them for dry cleaning. I was insulted and angry when I detected a fragrance I didn't recognize. Our vows screamed at me and reminded me of sacred promises that had been broken so many times, I feared they couldn't be salvaged. I knew how Humpty Dumpty felt as he lay broken and fragmented, witnessing the futility of the efforts demonstrated by royalty's servants.

Contrary to Carter's beliefs, quiet affairs didn't exist. They shouted at me and made me feel inadequate and insignificant. The more I tried to love him, the deeper his rejection hurt. The paranoia of another woman's confessions escalated with every hang-up phone call or private whisper I pretended not to hear. His samplings seemed to exist on an ever-changing carousel. Some nights when Carter climbed in bed, I could smell the other women on him. The cheating had to stop, or I was going to leave. I wanted to confront him. Instead, I laid beside him in silence, waiting for my courage to percolate to the surface. It never happened. I couldn't take it much longer. It was time to speak up.

When we married, I'd never envisioned our bond getting weaker, not stronger. The dry season from love I experienced in the midst of my marriage was heartbreaking. I deserved better. I decided I'd had enough. Because we didn't have children yet, starting over would be easier. I packed my bags and placed them by the front door, hoping to be swayed from leaving by a kernel of kindness and words of remorse from my husband. I wanted him to fight for me to stay and prove our marriage still mattered to him.

When Carter saw my suitcases, the surprised look on his face quickly changed to anger. My visual ultimatum was viewed as blatantly disrespectful. After all, he'd done for me, I didn't have the right to walk out on him. That's how he explained it as he landed the first blow. I wasn't quick enough to escape his wrath. It felt like ten hands were tattooing my body as I moved lifelessly around the room like a broken marionette. My legs didn't go behind my head when I landed. I was lucky. Each time he knocked me down, he picked me up, scolded me, and knocked me down again. Broken lamps added shards of glitter to the floor that became embedded in my hands and knees as I crawled away in desperation. He yanked my leg and pulled me back toward him. His shoes found a pathway across the middle of my back and on the nape of my neck. A shower of garments rained down on me from suitcases filled with possessions he claimed he owned. When the shower ended, an empty suitcase landed on top of me. I breathed a sigh of relief when he left the house and slammed the door behind him. I'd been mentally and physically crushed.

As I laid in bed recovering from the assault, I thought about something my mother told me years ago about control and bosom banks. *"Always put a little something away and out of sight from your mate and never lose your independence in a marriage."* I smiled when I thought about the visits with my grandma. She would reach into her bra, her bosom bank, and pull out money like a magic trick. I vowed to invest in a modern version of the concept but never did. There was no need, Carter took care of everything and always gave me money, even when I didn't ask for it. It was time to start acting on my mother's words.

My body tensed up when I heard Carter open the bedroom door. I held my breath until he laid down and snuggled up to me in bed, reeking of alcohol and spouting remorse. I allowed him to place his head on my chest. With bandaged hands, I stroked his shoulder and the side of his face until he fell asleep. He didn't feel the tears I deposited in his hair when I acknowledged I had nothing of my own. It felt like he owned me. All was right with his world; nothing was right in mine. The next time I packed my suitcases, I vowed to be long gone before he got home.

Chapter Twenty-Nine

Love Jones

Over the next two years, our marriage continued to limp along on life support. I didn't know marriage was supposed to feel so lonely. The love promises expressed through vows never fully bloomed. I'd watched my parent's expressions of love and wanted to share the same closeness with my husband. I didn't want to be able to tell where he ended and I began. I wanted him to look at me with eyes filled with love and a smile so bright it made the stars jealous. What I got from Carter was nowhere near that. Everywhere I turned, there was always a roadblock between me and his love. Although I stalked it, its elusive spirit always remained beyond my grasp. I wanted to feel good about the love that was supposed to encompass me. I never found those soft places to land where I was completely surrounded by the love of my husband. I mostly felt the stone-cold concrete of rejection.

Love continued to offend me. The hope of being loved, raised my expectations, then broke my heart. But even with a cracked heart, the love I had for Carter didn't completely leak out. The lack of love caused me to become love-obsessed. I knew there were no substitutes for it. I'd tried to wear them, collect them, pay for them, decorate them, drive them, and lie for them. I'd known how good it felt to be loved during my early days with Carter. Because of that, I suffered from an industrial-strength love hangover. It was like I drank a love potion for which there was no cure. I had a hunger and an unquenched desire for love that I didn't get from my husband. Each time I sat at the table of affection, I left unfulfilled. I often compared myself to a dog circling a table of affection, waiting for scraps to fall. All the little pieces and nibbles of affection didn't add up to enough to sustain me; I needed more. I had a love jones for my husband. All I needed from Carter was love, but it became the distant cousin I met long ago and would have trouble recognizing.

I marveled at how love changes people. Whether you have it and when you don't, a lasting impression is imprinted on your soul. I didn't love everything about Carter, but I loved him. Maybe I loved the person I thought he could be, and I kept waiting to see the one he portrayed when we first met. My eternal optimism about my marriage was often dashed by his unpredictable interaction patterns with me. Some days he treated me like he loved me; other days, I didn't exist. The hieroglyphic composition of his love language made it impossible for me to understand why he didn't seem interested in mine. Love couldn't thrive under those circumstances. It needs nurturing and constant reinforcement for it to reach its fullest potential.

Maybe love would've had a chance to grow had he only planted his seeds in my garden. The impact of his infidelities never seemed to go away. That was one of the unfortunate side effects of years of disappointments. Asking Carter to change and recommit to our marriage would have been a waste of words. I know. I tried. Even during the good times, it seemed the other woman was always between us caressing his skin as she bruised mine. She prevented our bodies from truly connecting in a complete marital union. Her scent burned my nostrils as my body failed to react to his raptured moans. I often wondered who he thought was underneath him as his passion spilled from his body. I didn't want to know if my face startled him back into reality, so I closed my eyes and allowed myself to be the face of whoever he wanted until he opened them again. Being needed by him was enough.

I heard that love gives itself away. I believed that if I gave my love to him, I would get it back with dividends. My logic abandoned me. My love was homeless.

Chapter Thirty

Angry Love

When I looked at my childhood viewpoint of how I thought my life would go, it included a nice home, expensive car, happy children, and the perfect man to make all my dreams come true. When my dreams didn't hold up their end of the bargain, the prophetic words of my mother mocked me. I'd heard what she said but didn't listen.

"Grace, always make sure you have a way to take care of yourself. You could be in the same house with a man, and he does nothing for you but makes sure you have a roof over your head without showing respect for you."

That's what it felt like being married to Carter.

Marriage was not a surface level commitment to me. I internalized every word of our vows within my soul. When I thought about the love and joy that surrounded us at our wedding ceremony, I was happy to live up to the marriage promises we made. I couldn't say the same about Carter. He solemnly pledged to forsake all others and keep himself only for me, but he acted like his fingers were crossed behind his back during that portion of the ceremony. He'd repeated the wedding vows with passion, but no meaning. The rings we'd given each other represented a promise of fidelity and eternal love. It still bothered me that he never wore his wedding band. The outward symbol of our union and the depth of his devotion to our vows remained hidden from the world like a CIA secret.

Each time was promised to be the last infidelity episode. If I'd change how I did this or not say that, he'd work on our marriage. I changed. He faked it. Carter would eventually go back to itching for other female companionship, and I would pretend I still mattered. Somewhere down the line, I settled for less and less. Once I acknowledged the love I'd expected to savor for a lifetime was fading, I focused on cashing in on the benefits package that came along with this relationship. That rationale wasn't enough for me. I wanted what was promised on our wedding day. I had to figure out how to get some of that back.

I thought about how we'd settled problems in our family. One of my father's favorite saying was "I'm not a mind reader. Just because you think it, doesn't mean I know it. You've gotta open your mouth and say what's on your mind if you want to be heard." Maybe our solution was better communication. We couldn't fix anything if we didn't talk. I couldn't remember the last time we'd had meaningful, unfiltered dialogue about us. I was ready to talk about how we could make our marriage stronger and explore the possibility of starting a family. We needed to get our closeness back before we added children to our world.

A dinner filled with forced conversations and hardly any eye contact was indicative of the communication concerns I had about our troubled marriage. My intentions were pure when I sat down with Carter and shared what was on my heart.

"Carter, I think we need to talk."

"Okay. I'll play along. What exactly do you want to talk about?"

"Us. We're not close anymore. We barely talk, and we hardly ever go out. You're gone all the time and when you're here, you don't make time for me. You barely touch me anymore. You lay beside me, but I can tell your mind is somewhere else."

"Where is all this coming from, Grace?"

"I'm scared of where our marriage is heading. Have I done something? Just tell me what's wrong, and we can fix it. A couple of months ago, we talked about starting a family. If we don't get us back, it would be unfair to complicate things further with children."

"Look, we're ok. I know I've been preoccupied lately, but don't worry about it. I'm just going through some things at work. What do you think I need to do to make things better?"

"Number one, you have to stop hitting me while you're angry. Sometimes, it feels like you're punishing me for what someone else has done. I don't deserve that. You promised my father you'd never hurt me like that. Don't you love me anymore?"

"I get it, Grace. My anger gets the best of me, sometimes."

"You always take your anger out on me. You hurt me all the time. A couple of times you've beaten me so badly that I couldn't walk. You've broken my wrist, knocked out teeth, nearly busted my eardrum, given me black eyes, busted lips, bloody noses, bruises all over my body, and you claim you love me. That's not love, Carter. That's abuse. I love you, but that has to stop. One day you are gonna hurt me in ways that I can't hide with clothing, make-up, and lies."

"Okay, baby, I promise I will stop hitting you in anger."
"Thank you."

"Like I said, we're fine, Grace. Is that all?"

"No, Carter, we're not fine, not as long as these women keep calling our home looking for you. How do you think that makes me feel? Why don't you ever want to acknowledge my feelings?"

"Here we go again. Grace, please. Let's talk about something else. You can't keep living in the past."

"Maybe it's the past for you, but not for me. I've never been able to leave it behind. I'm stuck. How can I leave it behind when I'm constantly getting hurt? The other night when you claimed to be working late, you weren't. I came to your office. I wanted to surprise you. You weren't there. I called, but you didn't answer."

"Are you spying on me now? I had a dinner meeting. I don't think I need to report my movements to you. You're my wife, not my mother. I'm a grown man."

"Yes, you're a grown, married man. I think you forget that sometimes."

I knew when I said that, I'd gone too far. I could see the rage building in his eyes. I was afraid. When he drew back his fist to hit me, I cowered away with my hands in a protective position in front of my face and yelled, "No, Carter. Not again. You promised."

Carter dropped his hand, turned his back to me, and walked toward our bedroom. I breathed a sigh of relief and sat down on the couch. I was happy to see him honoring his recent promise. Three minutes later, Carter reappeared with a belt wrapped around his hand. Everything faded into the background as I watched him move closer and closer to me with it held high above his head. My backward movement on the sofa could only get me as far as the corner between the arm and the backrest. I braced myself for the first downward movement. I heard its swooshing sound before it made contact with my skin. Each time he struck me, it felt like a swarm of bees was stinging my body. I could feel the swelling of my skin as it reacted to the coarse leather. I couldn't ball myself up small enough to escape the merging of his anger and my flesh. I'd never been whipped as a child and never thought I'd face that type of degradation as an adult, married woman. Several times as he landed blows, he yelled at me but called me by his mother's name. The beating went on for several minutes. I attempted to kick him in his groin as my legs and feet peddled an imaginary bicycle, and my hands grabbed for the belt. The closest I got to that target was his upper thigh and the glass of the coffee table.

That only made him madder. My hands and breast area paid the price before I retreated into a ball again and prayed and cried throughout the remainder of the flogging. After he'd physically exhausted his anger, Carter flung the belt across the room and sat down on the other end of the sofa with his head in his hands, trying to control his heavy breathing. It was finally over. I'd been sufficiently punished.

I staggered into the bathroom and locked the door behind me. My whole body felt like it was on fire. I removed my clothes and looked at the welts on my body. Overlapping marks formed red crisscrossed patterns on my back and arms, the most exposed areas. They reminded me of exaggerated mosquito bites, slightly larger than the width of his belt. They hurt worse than they looked. Those surface-level marks cut deep into my soul.

The hot water from the shower scorched my skin along the path of his anger. I stood there in agony. If I wanted to experience its healing properties, I couldn't pull back. As the compounded pain of abuse and degradation coursed through my body, the face of my father popped into my head. I longed to be my daddy's little girl again. I wanted to feel safe, loved, and protected by a man who would never intentionally hurt me. After getting out of the shower, I took a good look in the full-length mirror at blistered stripes on my body. Unacceptable. It was settled. As soon as I got to the bedroom, I was going to call my father. I'd had enough. My body reflected how mentally and physically vicious Carter's attack had been. I didn't care what my father did to him. I would have welcomed cutting him six ways instead of five.

When I walked out of the bathroom, I didn't expect Carter to be sitting on my side of the bed. He never said a word before he walked over to me, removed my towel, and started to kiss the raised places on my skin. I had no physical response as he eased my naked body onto the bed and gently ran his fingers along the welts. When the weight of his body pressed down on mine, I wanted to scream until he got off me. I couldn't speak or cry; I was in shock. All I could do was look up at the ceiling while my mind escaped to a place far from the spot I laid. It was calm and free. It remained detached from reality while his body moved toward his carnal goal. When the familiar snoring sound reached my ear, I hung my head over the side of the bed and vomited.

The next morning, I wanted nothing to do with him. I pretended to be asleep when Carter left for work. I was too repulsed to look him in the eye. After careful consideration, I talked to my father but couldn't ask him to rescue me. I didn't want to hear the pain in his voice or be responsible for a murder. I just wanted a hug from him in my ear. After I finished that conversation, I called Carter's mother. She agreed to meet me for lunch the next time he was away on business. I needed the time to process the information I hoped to obtain. I wanted to understand who he was and how deeply his anger was rooted. Hopefully, I would know soon.

Chapter Thirty-One

Bloodlines

I often wondered what was at the root ball of the pain that bubbled up through fissures of anger trapped within my husband. I wanted to understand why he exhibited a lack of love and kindness toward me. It was amazing how he could attach and detach himself emotionally from me as easily as flipping a light switch. I believe the anger he carried around was packed deep in generational scars he was forced to inherit and pay forward. When he was abusive, he detached himself from culpability and never shouldered his burden from the harm he caused. Sometimes I thought I was being punished because he didn't know how to love. Other times I felt it was his way to control me. I believed there was a better side of Carter that he kept hidden from me. Hopefully, his mother would give me directions on how to find it and provide insight into the childhood he never talked about.

The atmosphere at the restaurant was light and festive, quite the opposite of our topic of conversation. I didn't know how to bring up the subject of Carter's abuse to his mother. I didn't want to see the pain in her eyes from revelation or the guilt from confirmation. Mrs. Mann made it easy for me when she said, "Grace, I know you invited me to lunch to discuss my son. Let me guess, he's physically abusing you."

I timidly confirmed her suspicion when I said, "Yes, ma'am." When we looked in each other's eyes, mine indicated shame, while her eyes communicated guilt and concern for me.

Mrs. Mann didn't mince words when she said, "Grace, you seem like an intelligent girl. You even have a college degree. Why haven't you left my son yet?"

Her bluntness surprised me. "Because I love him," I responded, but wanted to say, "Duh!"

She thought for a while then said, "One day, that won't be enough. Then, what will you do? What will be your reason for staying with him, and what will be the reason you eventually decide to leave?"

I cleared my throat and took a sip of my water as I searched for an answer to questions I'd never considered. I was relieved when she started to share parts of her family's history.

"How much has my son told you about his father?"

"Not much. He was really general when my father asked about him."

"I could see why he didn't want to talk about him much. Carter is so much like his father, who was not the type of man I wanted my son to be. My husband was vicious and unforgiving one minute, loving and generous the next. When he found out I was pregnant, you couldn't remove the smile from his face each time he expressed his desire for a son. During my pregnancy, he kept his hands to himself and resorted to verbal abuse. It stung but was a welcome compromise."

"I prayed many times for a girl. I believed I could protect her more, and she wouldn't become an angry rendition of her father. I always wondered what my life would've been like with a daughter. More than likely, he would've wanted me to keep having babies until I produced another male to carry on the bloodline. I wouldn't dare bring another child into the horror of our marriage. Then I would have to worry about the survival of two children and myself."

She paused long enough for the waiter to serve our meal before she continued to unfold her history with Carter's father. "Like it is for most men, Carter was my husband's dream. His desire for our son to become someone who would carry on the family name and legacy became my greatest fear. For years, I was able to shield his eyes from the abuse until the day Carter walked in and saw his father beating me with a belt because dinner wasn't ready when he got home. Mind you, I worked a full-time job, too, but that didn't matter. I left our home the next day. After six months of his begging in one ear and my mother's voice in the other, I went back home. I regret it to this day. The only reason I went back was for Carter. I wanted to protect his heart from being hurt by not being around his father. What a mistake."

I squirmed when she mentioned the belt. That revelation hit too close to home. I was only three weeks removed from my leather belt incident. I never wanted to be brutalized and humiliated like that ever again. I understood why he said her name. He learned that trick from his father.

"I always prayed and wondered if the sacrifice I made for my son was enough. I questioned if I'd loved the evil part of his father out of him. For a while, I thought I'd saved him. One day, one of his girlfriend's parents paid me a visit. I knew I'd failed. I didn't protect him. I couldn't even protect myself," she said before she took a sip of her coffee.

After hearing that portion of her story, I thought, "What an awful burden to have carried all these years. She's not responsible for the acts of a grown man. Carter does those things to me because he wants to. Not being loved enough wasn't his problem."

I saw the fear in her eyes when she asked, "Do you plan to have children?"

"We've talked about it. Why do you ask?"

117

"Fatherhood didn't fix my husband, Grace. It calmed him down during my pregnancy, but as you know, that was a temporary solution. Please think twice about having his children."

"But I want to be a mother, and I'm sure you want to be a grandmother. That's all my mother talks about. I've always wanted at least two children. I couldn't imagine having grown up without my sister. I want that same bond for my children."

Mrs. Mann looked at me and said, "Grace, I want you to repeat after me. Leopards and spots."

"Okay. Leopards and spots."

Then she said, "No matter how you dress them up, you will always be able to recognize one by their spots. They can't change. Do you understand what I'm saying, Grace?"

I nodded my head. I understood what she meant, but I wasn't ready to believe he couldn't change. While standing outside the restaurant, Carter's mother left me with a few things to consider when she said, "Grace, you're a lovely girl, and I want to give you a bit of advice. I wouldn't blame you if you left him, but please protect yourself if you stay. He's my son, and I love him, but he's too angry for you. You deserve better."

After I visited with Carter's mother, his cheating became more frequent and blatant than ever before. So did his abuse. I understood him better, but nothing I did kept him happy or kept me out of danger. I needed relief. Carter's mother had surreptitiously planted seeds of a solution in my mind that I decided to harvest. It didn't take much for me to convince him it was time we started a family. I believe he harbored guilt about the loss of our first child and wanted to make amends. We actively pursued parenthood and were both overjoyed to announce our pregnancy. I wasn't there when he broke the news to his mother, but I could imagine the turmoil she felt on the inside.

Over the course of my pregnancy, Carter didn't abuse me physically, but he continued to cheat. Risking our baby's health for his own pleasure was completely selfish, but not surprising. I didn't know why I expected him to deviate from his behavior patterns. During my last trimester, he stayed closer to home and didn't stray as much. Maybe the thought of fatherhood became more of a reality. Whatever the catalyst was, I was glad that he was there with me.

I was thrilled when my first bundle of joy and protection arrived. I remember lying in the hospital bed, observing his joy at the birth of our son. The pride bled through his eyes as he held his child in his arms. I saw a different side of Carter when it came to his son, CJ, and I hoped that version of him would remain. I remember telling myself that I knew he would love me now; I'd borne him a son. Since I gave him the heir he wanted, I wouldn't get hurt again. Six months after our son was born, his anger returned. Neither one of us fully understood how exhausting it would be to care for an infant. The baby required a lot of my time, especially since I was breastfeeding. He was clueless about what it took to care for a small child. His work shielded him from the rigors of parenthood. When he got home, CJ was fed, his dinner was cooked, and I was ready for a nap. He often commented about feeling left out and neglected by the lack of attention. I was giving the baby more than I was giving him, and it was taking some time for my lingerie to make an appearance. Ironically, it took him three months to want out of the shoes of neglect I'd worn for several years. As soon as I noticed his anger ramping up after each whiny conversation about his needs, I knew the abuse wouldn't be too far behind. Three months later, I was pregnant again.

When our daughter, Taylor, was born, a softer side of him emerged. He was two different people when it came to his daughter and me. Just like me, she was daddy's girl. He adored her and lavished love on her without hesitation. I understood the importance of that relationship and appreciated the special bond Carter was building with our daughter. But I wanted to feel special too. As soon as Taylor could recognize his voice, he called throughout the day to talk to her. He'd always say, "How's daddy's favorite girl?" Her face would light up when she held the phone to her ear. She often met him at the door so he could pick her up and swing her around in circles. Carter was always bringing her gifts and spent more time with her than he did with me and CJ. I hoped some of the gentleness he expressed toward his daughter would linger around long enough to find its way to me. I almost felt jealous when I thought about how she got so much from him, and I got so little.

Even though our children represented a way for me to be loved again, it was not the love I was pining for. I wanted more than parental love had to offer. I wanted my husband to love me. I wanted him to be mesmerized by me and adored to the same degree and beyond what he felt for our children. I wanted him to look to me only for his physical needs. I ended up wanting a lot of things I didn't get.

As the babies got older, I thought being the mother of his children would give me reduced susceptibility to his physical abuse outbursts. I was wrong. I learned not to scream as loudly and plead more quietly once they were safely tucked in bed and soundly sleeping. I was convinced that I could successfully hide my injuries from my friends and family, but I wondered what my children saw. Did they notice the times I winced when reaching above my head to retrieve supplies from the kitchen cabinets, or when I couldn't give them a hug or even pick them up when outstretched arms were presented when they needed comfort from me? Would they remember the times I struggled to not cry out in pain when one of them playfully jumped into bed with me and inadvertently brushed up against some unsealed part of my being? Just like Carter's mother, I had fears of who they would become and the influence their father would be in their lives. They were the ones I needed to fight for the most. The thought of mirroring our dysfunction in front of our children filled me with shame each time I thought about my selfish motives toward motherhood. I hadn't solved any problems, I'd created more.

Chapter Thirty-Two

Common Ground

"This just in from the WRPE news desk. Pre-trial motions are being heard today by the judge presiding over the Carter Mann assault case. Because of the publicity resulting from this high-profile defendant, a motion for change of venue and suppression of evidence will be presented. We will keep you updated as more information becomes available."

The longer Carter remained behind bars, the more his financial secrets were revealed. His portfolio was extensive and diversified, just as he'd told my father. All the bank accounts, investments, and real estate holdings told the story of my source of economic freedom. My mother once advised me to at least get a part-time job so that I could have a feeling of independence. My part-time job had become caring for myself after Carter's attacks. It didn't pay well but the amount in my bosom bank filled me with pride. In it, I squirreled away pieces from my monthly stipend, my household budget, and expensive gifts I returned. Having that secret stash made me feel good about myself. It wasn't millions of dollars, but it was mine. To me, I was rich. I had something I'd done for myself that fostered a growing sense of independence.

I settled into my new role as a decision-maker with ease. I welcomed the change. Questionable expenditures ended with my instructions to the accountant, and all credit card statements were sent for my approval. Among the papers in Carter's locked drawers were files with names, addresses, and phone numbers of several women. I was fascinated by how detailed they were and was glad there were no pictures. Some of the addresses corresponded with real estate holdings in his portfolio. I saw the address of the apartment he rented for me and smirked. He'd owned that property two years before I moved in. Why was I surprised? As I dug further, I saw Eva's information. I hoped the phone number was still good.

My anxiety heightened each time the phone rang without being answered. On the fourth ring, a gentle voice said, "Hello."

"Eva, it's Grace." I paused and allowed my name to register.

An emotionless, "Hi," was her response, followed by silence.

I cleared my throat and said, "I was wondering if you wanted to go out for a cup of coffee."

Without giving her a chance to respond, I said, "I would understand if you said no." To my surprise, her answer was yes.

In my mind, calling Eva was the craziest thing I'd done in many years. I didn't know what kept motivating me to communicate with her. Our first meeting was orchestrated by my husband. I did it for him. This meeting was just for me. I wanted to learn more about the woman who exhibited such strength of character when we first met. Maybe some of her courage would rub off on me.

During the ride to the coffee house, my mind wandered back to Eva's mother's protective stance in the hospital. I wondered if she knew about my invitation and if she tried to convince Eva not to entertain my request. I wondered if Eva would even show up. And what was that knife comment all about? Maybe one day, Eva would explain. There were many streets where I could have turned around between my house and the coffee shop. The closer I got to the meeting place, the more anxious I became. I saw her sitting by the window as I approached. Eva waved and acknowledged my presence. I couldn't read her expression as she welcomed me into the chair opposite hers. There was no turning back now.

At first, it was awkward looking into the face of the woman who could easily be considered a homewrecker. But I knew that was not completely true. I'd been living in a slow-motion disaster of a marriage for more years than I tried to forget. I didn't believe I could move fast enough in the opposite direction to get away from what I knew would have a tragic ending. Carter wrecked our home years ago. Eva had been one in a line of either victims or fools. For the most obvious reasons, I put her in the victim category.

Thank God for the coffee mug. It provided somewhere for me to focus my nervous energy as I searched for my words.

"Thank you for agreeing to meet with me. I know this seems odd."

"Yes. That's what my mother said. She told me to be careful around you."

"I understand why she would be concerned."

"I'm sure she is somewhere close by." My expression changed to one of concern. Eva laughed, then said, "No, she's not. She's at home with Joy."

Eva smiled as she watched relief wash over my face. I managed to take a sip of coffee without spilling it on myself.

The focus of our conversation drifted to a subject that would forever bond us together, Joy. Eva spoke with pride about the love of her life. She proudly displayed recent photos and talked lovingly about her daughter. I understood how her child's name represented the perpetual admiration for her existence.

I decided that I wanted to understand Eva's life further before she met Carter. I wanted to see if our resemblance and my husband were the only traits we shared.

"Eva, did you grow up with a father?"

"For part of my life. He died when I was young."

"That must have been hard."

"It was, but I had my Big Daddy to fill in the gap. I feel as though I had two of the finest examples of men in my life."

I watched Eva's eyes shine with admiration as she talked about her most influential male role models.

"What about you? Is your father still alive?"

"Yes."

The tone of her voice changed when she said, "And he ain't shot Ben yet for hurting you?"

Although her response was somewhat comical, she wasn't smiling. I didn't offer an explanation.

Eva continued her childhood memory. "When my Big Daddy first met Adam, he came outside and sat on the porch with a rifle. It scared him and me half to death." She smiled at the memory then said, "He took Adam for a walk around our property and questioned him like he was in court. He was sweating so bad that it looked like he had on a sweat necklace." She smiled at the memory then said, "I overheard him tell my Big Mama one day that his family wasn't worth two dead flies."

Eva laughed with her whole being as she thought about the plight of her childhood beau. Her amusement was infectious, and we both reveled in that moment of lightness. When the laughter ended, she said, "But from day one, Adam knew Big Daddy meant business. I don't know what they talked about during their walk, but Adam told me that Big Daddy made it clear that he better not ever put his hands on me in anger."

I paused before I spoke, "My father doesn't know about the abuse." After I said those words, I took a deep breath and looked down in shame at the liquid inside my coffee cup. I'd never admitted that to anyone except Carter's mother. I braced for the impact, but nothing happened. The sky didn't fall, the world didn't spin off its axis, my chair didn't get sucked into a black hole, and my lips didn't fall off. When I looked up from my cup, the morality police weren't standing by ready to imprison me, and Eva didn't look down on me. Suddenly, the fear of releasing those words into the universe seemed unwarranted. Space in my crowded soul was freed up with my confession as years of dead weight was released.

"Come again? Are you sure about that? Trust me, they know. I could look into your eyes and see that you had been abused by Ben. Your demeanor reminded me of my mother's after my father passed. She wasn't abused. She was broken from sadness. That same type of loss and frailty showed through your eyes. You don't think your family sees that too?"

I was glad that Eva kept referring to that "Ben" character. I didn't know him. As long as she called him Ben, I could keep him separate from the person I knew and loved. I could preserve the feelings I had for Carter that clung to me like an errant spider web.

Eva took a sip of coffee and said, "Grace, can I ask you something?"

"Sure."

"After he hit you the first time, why did you stay?"

"Because I loved him, and I thought he would never do it again. At least that's what he promised. That promise lasted until he got angry again, and I became the scapegoat."

"I understand. We got into a big argument one time, and he slapped me across the face. I wore his handprint for days. He made that same promise and apology, and I continued to see him."

I sat quietly and listened to an abbreviated biopsy of my early years with Carter. I could have inserted my name into

126

her story. I understood the escalation patterns and the explosion, followed by his remorse. The anatomy of his actions was the same. Like his mother said, "Leopards and spots."

I tried to justify my reasons for staying with Carter by responding, "I never thought about how it felt to stand in my family's shoes. I was too ashamed and too afraid to tell anyone about it. I loved him and wanted my family to like him too. I wanted them to see the good things I saw in him. Besides, he didn't hit me all the time. Only when he lost control. It wasn't that bad."

I let that statement linger in the air and almost cringed when I thought about what I just said. I was sure Eva saw right through the lie. She had intimate knowledge of how bad he could be when he lost control. I didn't know if I was trying to convince myself or her when I said, "Every couple goes through things in a relationship. I didn't want to ruin everything because of a misunderstanding, especially after we made up. You know how it is." I was trying to convince myself. Otherwise, I would have to admit how broken and detached from his abuse I'd become. I was sure Eva could see me floundering in my pain and allowed me to retain some of my dignity. She reached over and patted my hands, as if to say, "It's not your fault." We both sat in extended silence until she asked, "Did your Father like Ben?"

"No, my Daddy was not too fond of him and told me not to think glass was diamonds. Carter reminded him of his Uncle Charles, who couldn't keep his hands to himself when he got angry."

"Umph. Ain't that something. My mother didn't like him either the first time she met him. She said he was artificial. I didn't listen to her, either."

Eva's words hung in the air and caused me to reflect on my father's reaction to Carter. It made me nod in silent affirmation as I replayed my father's words in my mind. He knew something was off after spending one evening with him. So, did I, but his means, which included a lucrative career and an upgraded lifestyle for me, outweighed the smell of danger. I couldn't help but think of where my life would've been had I listened to my father. All I wanted to focus on was the love I thought I'd get from Carter.

"Grace, you should never underestimate the love of your family and how far they will go to protect you. My mother gave a man her version of a vasectomy to defend my honor. You don't think your family would do the same for you? Well, not that same thing, but you know what I mean."

I was sure Eva could read my expression when the meaning of the knife comment became clear.

Eva continued, "I even thought about that myself the night I found out Ben was married. I stood over him with a knife in my hand, ready to separate his manhood from his body. But that's a story for another day."

I gasped, then thought, "That same adultery remedy had crossed my mind a couple of times. Something else we have in common."

We talked for a few more minutes before Eva said, "Look at the time. I've gotta get home. I don't want my mother to come looking for you with her knife." We both laughed as we exited the coffee shop. Our meeting had gone well. I hoped that we could talk again.

On the way home, I thought a lot about what Eva said about family. When my family first saw the formation of subtle cracks and an unidentifiable imbalance, they tried to intervene. They saw the me I tried to hide. After rebuffing their initial attempts to save me from Carter, they stopped trying. In my mind, they stopped caring, as well. Clearly, I'd underestimated them. They had supported me unconditionally since Carter's arrest. The problem hadn't been with them, it was with me. I had so much more to learn about being a parent.

Chapter Thirty-Three

Insanity

I longed for, but did not get, the kindness I thought everyone deserved from their partner. The dreams and fantasies I envisioned in my youth withered away under the pressure of reality. Even so, my heart kept trying to save the day. It told my eyes what to see and had them looking in a direction far removed from the truth of my existence. Once they refocused, they cried alone and produced droplets no one ever saw. When signs of weakness spilled over the edge of my resolve, I made sure they evaporated as quickly as morning dew on a summer's day. I couldn't show signs of defeat even though the loneliness was crushing me from every direction. It felt like I was trying to support the weight of our marriage in the middle of my chest. I could barely breathe. I needed relief.

With the amount of time I spent alone, I didn't feel married. Carter's separate life had gone on so long that I became immune to the indiscretions that plagued a large portion of our marriage. For my sanity, I'd diverted my focus and accepted what I decided were arbitrary forays into infidelity. That mindset awakened the demons that skulked around in the midst of the quiet on nights I was home alone. They ridiculed me, pointed out my marital inferiority, and hurled names that pierced the shell of my resolve. I wilted under the weight of words I allowed them to drape over me. There was no escape. My only hope was to let darkness calm me and close my ears to the sounds of disappointments. But that was only temporary as my inner thoughts were overtaken by the repetitive words and faces I longed to forget.

My life was unraveling like a string on a hem. I didn't want to pull it too hard. I feared I wouldn't be able to put it back together if it came totally apart. For a long time, I was content with the life I'd accepted. I could make do. I wasn't happy but I wasn't miserable, either. There were even times when life was good. Since I couldn't figure out how I could amputate the bad from my life without damaging the good, those good memories became my anchor. But no matter how much I avoided it, the ugly truth always found its way back to me. It was all around, permeating my aura with the tension of what was bound to return to my life. The cycle never ended. It kept me on edge and never allowed me to experience peace. I kept doing and allowing the same things to happen over and over, time after time, wishing for a different outcome. It was the classic definition of insanity. Carter made attempts to spend more time at home, but before long, the itch that needed scratching returned, followed by the smell of foreign perfume, random phone calls, elevated credit card bills, and heartache.

I never wanted to get caught by the truth. I ran like Forrest Gump, only no one put up the stop sign for me. I wanted to stay free from turmoil and stay wrapped in the cloak of mediocrity's garments. I could continue to accept the nothingness of isolation and regret as I clothed my body and soul in the fabric of overpriced designers. I settled for the expression of his love through credit cards. Even with my economic liberties, I felt like dried-up dung that would eventually blow away at the next unexpected gust. I had to use a lot of cologne to cover the stench that constantly swirled around me. That was my prize for the man I had wrestled away from a woman who had staked her claim years before me. I wonder if she's thanking me now.

There were times when I felt useless and considered myself a total failure as a wife. I sat around like a potted plant, waiting for the moisture of validation from Carter to rain on me. I ended up withering away and losing damaged pieces of myself because of neglect. I relied heavily on my survival kit of makeup to cover my bruises, time to believe it would all get better and denial to cover my delusions. That level of passivity kept me living through an infinite loop of the scenes from the worst B-movie I'd ever seen with the most unoriginal plot in the world.

"From the world of Carter Mann comes the riveting new film about old behaviors. The story begins when Boy meets girl. Girl likes boy. Boy has another girl. After a few months, Girl wins boy. Boy marries girl. And for the next few years, Boy finds another girl. Girl finds out. Girl is heartbroken. Boy apologizes to Girl. Girl forgives boy. Girl stays with boy. To no one's surprise, Boy finds more girls. Girl confronts boy. Boy hits girl. Girl forgives boy. Boy lies to girl. Girl finds out. Boy finds new girls. Girl still loves boy. Girl doesn't love herself. As we move closer to the climax, you guessed it, Boy meets another girl. But wait, this girl is different. Get ready for an ending no one will ever forget!"

This had been overdone too many times for it to have an impact, or so I thought. But I knew how original and captivating the saga was for those in the midst of such life-altering situations. When the credits rolled, I saw my name listed below Carter's. He was the star, but I helped produce the content. It was a masterpiece for which I shamefully took part of the credit. My gut always told me when auditions were being held for the remake. I knew it wouldn't be long before it was time for more coke and popcorn. Maybe I would splurge on extra butter. Sooner or later I expected a plot twist; Boy impregnates another girl.

Chapter Thirty-Four

Jump

Carter's continued mental and physical abuse changed everything; not only for him but also for what it was doing to me and the children. The more time he spent away from home, the more like a single parent I felt. It crippled me in more ways than I could have imagined. As the toxicity level in our marriage elevated, I became the perfect wife he longed for me to be; submissive, quiet, and afraid.

There were times when I questioned if my sanity and resolve could withstand another round of his warped sense of love and kindness. I spent so much time recovering but not healing. The cycle of abuse showed no signs it would stop. It became a routine I got comfortable with: Beat. Apologize. Hide. Heal. Repeat. The emptiness always returned after the hugs and attention subsided, and the external bruising was no longer noticeable. He would show me the attention I longed for and I would reset my tolerance meter. I wasn't sure I knew what it felt like to be loved.

Except for my children, very few things brought me joy any more. I was miserable. I had no control over my own life. He manipulated my thoughts, reactions, and movements. He consumed all of me until I was just skin and bones—a skeleton encased in skin being propelled by shattered hopes and dreams. I was always unbalanced. Each time I tried to stand up, he knocked me back down, either with his words or his actions. The spigot of pain never turned off. Even when I thought it ended, droplets of humiliation caused gravity to continue fueling the leaks in my self-esteem. I was too paralyzed by fear to do or say very much. I couldn't count the number of times my words were swallowed for the sake of remaining safe and unbruised. Fists, guns, and belts made lasting impressions on me.

Beyond the physical abuse was the domineering incapacitation of mental abuse. As much as the physical stings left marks on my body, the mental abuse left scars on my soul. At times I preferred the finite discomfort of physical catastrophes. With mental abuse, the pain inflicted from his spiteful words caused constant uneasiness long after they were spoken. They recycled through my mind and expanded in depth each time I allowed them to be recalled. As long as I could think, the residue lingered, waiting to be revived to disrupt any feelings of normalcy that were brave enough to try to take root. I hated to admit that my journey to the path I traveled taught me a lesson about stealing. I learned the hard way that sometimes what you take isn't worth keeping. I wanted what someone else had so badly that I never stopped to think about their feelings. The green grass I saw on Carter's side of the fence turned out to be AstroTurf. I'd fertilized it with my dignity and watered it with my blood. Still, it wouldn't grow. Many times, I wished I could throw him back over the fence. During those times, I heard karma laughing in my ear as it called out the corresponding numbers of the Ten Commandments I'd broken.

During some of his physical attacks, Carter lost full control. It was as if he was having an out-of-body experience, using someone else's evil mind. I often wished I could cry until the tears flowing from my eyes turned to blood, and my heart had nothing left to pump. I didn't want a future if all I had to look forward to was more of the same. Once I was beaten so badly, I feared I was at the brink of death. I surrendered my will to live to the inevitable and I imagined the finality of free-falling from the highest building

I could find. Contentment surrounded my being as the coolness of the wind against my warm body produced vapor streams during my descent. I imagined myself looking in the windows at people whose faces changed too quickly to be recognizable. I closed my eyes and enjoyed the lightness I felt. I would be free soon. Nothing else could hurt me after the initial impact. When I felt I was getting close to the magic moment, I opened my eyes. The sidewalk became closer and closer as I fell faster and faster. I braced for the sudden impact. I took one last look to the left. There I saw the faces of my children. I reached for them in desperation as I called their names. They smiled. I lived.

Chapter Thirty-Five

Tolerance

Carter's absence from the home allowed me to look at the anatomy of our relationship. Peeling back the layers exposed my vulnerability to illusions. There were many nights when I laid in bed and thought about how I'd made it so easy for the glass to continue to look like diamonds. From the very beginning, I taught Carter how to treat me. He learned well. I allowed him to sow seeds of discord and never required him to suffer through the harvest of the tares and weeds. I stuffed down so much hurt because I didn't ask for what I needed. I just accepted what he gave without expressing my needs. Where my mouth should have been was a continual sea of skin rendering me speechless. I'd lost the power of my voice. Without it, I became nothing in front of him. It was befitting that he treated me like nothing. But I wouldn't complain. I didn't want to show anger toward him and be deprived of the morsels of affections he sporadically gave me. It was like throwing scraps to a hungry dog. How could the scraps be refused? I was willing to take whatever he gave and enjoy it. Those intermittent acts of kindness angered me but not enough to make me walk away. I was content that he still wanted me around.

In others, I saw glimpses of the life I wanted; a hopelessly ordinary life with my husband, children, and a home filled with love, the way I'd grown up. What I experienced was nowhere close. I'd been written a marital commitment check with disappearing ink. The first indiscretion wounded me to my core. The ones after that had less impact and over time, each successive cut didn't feel as deep and the wound didn't bleed as profusely. I went from feeling like the cut required surgery to it only requiring a Band-Aid. My mantra became who's next. I wondered if that was how his ex-fiancé felt when she found out about me.

The depth of faith and love for my husband caused me to believe in him and stick with him through all the lies and the crushing of my spirit. He didn't know what it was like to drag around his infidelity. It constantly pulled down on my soul like the cumulative weight of a cotton picker's bag. The longer we were married, the deeper the ruts became. They got so deep that I was ready to give up and lay down in the coolness of the shallow grave I dug. Even though it was hard, I found the strength to keep climbing back out of the same rut of dysfunction. It was harder than trying to put on that pair of Spanx I outgrew last year that squished me and made it hard to breathe. I was drowning in my Red Sea of sorrows, afraid I'd get swallowed up in the landscape of obscurity. Too many disappointments without remorse crossed our path and nothing but bad decisions remained in our wake.

Throughout our marriage, I kept waiting on a transplant of a consciousness to occur. No names ever appeared on the donor list. Togetherness no longer seemed a viable option, yet I was determined to hold on to a fantasy that died on the vine years earlier. Each time I thought I was at the end of my rope, he would let out just enough to keep me hanging around. I had callouses from all the times I kept that rope from choking me. I didn't know how much more of myself I could continue to lose and still be considered a whole person.

I kept forfeiting pieces of myself as the haunting soundtrack of mental and physical brutality played on. For as long as I could remember, that had been the roadmap in our marriage manual. No matter how small the perceived infraction, he went into hate mode and stayed there until he thought I was worthy enough to have the pleasure of a meaningful conversation. Having no interaction with the person that was the other half of me was worse than any physical assault he could inflict. At least with the physical degradation, it would be over after the pain subsided. I'd come to know the length of the healing process and how long to avoid my family. I would receive gifts, his veiled way of expressing sorrow, and our lives would go back to normal.

With the silent assault, I never knew how long it would last. He held his words hostage and didn't acknowledge I was in the room. That stung. Even when we were at the dinner table or riding in the car, no words were sent in my direction. If the children were in the car, he talked to them. I found it quite offensive that when we were at a social gathering, the words from his lips flowed like Niagara Falls; the laughter genuine. Even though he was dumb in my direction, I smiled when I thought I should, laughed at the supposed funny quips, and pretended it didn't matter. I knew not to use my words against him. To do so would be disastrous for my well-being. I patiently waited in silent protest until he deemed me worthy of his words again. When they returned, I received them with pasted smiles and lying eyes that emoted happiness when his silky baritone voice replaced the silence ringing in my ear.

There were times when I missed my husband, even while he was in the same house, occupying the space right next to me. He barely paid attention to me and I felt as arbitrary as the new comforter he pulled up under his neck. Any notions of intimacy were quarantined. I was hesitant to tell him how I wanted to be swept away with the passion of our first time; his breath in my body, his being in my being, our bodies and souls exposed and covered with desire. I wanted to see his eyes dance around my body, anticipating the places he would conquer and appreciate. I wanted to lay breathless beside him, inhaling his essence, as he moved the hair that partially covered my face. That's how we started, and I wanted that connection again.

Instead, I would lay there painfully aware that my expectations weren't grounded in reality. He often turned away from me and acted as if I didn't have emotional or physical desires that only he could fulfill. I never thought I'd have to practically beg my husband to make love to me. I viewed it as my way of holding on to my version of our love story. Without a physical connection, I felt deserted. Afterward, there was nothing. No cuddling, no kissing, no peace, no togetherness. Just his back to me. The next morning, I almost left payment for services rendered on my nightstand for the husband impersonator. The stranger I was living with was killing me slowly with his lack of affection. I seriously considered filing a missing person's report for the man I married. I realized that a commitment without love doesn't make a marriage. I could get that from a roommate, and I wouldn't feel obligated to kiss them in the mouth.

As the emotional distance between us grew wider, our marriage got weaker. It spelled more trouble. Our marriage quality reminded me of a helium-filled balloon that slipped through our fingers and was slowly moving further out of our reach. At times of desperation, I wanted to move to another city in hopes of a fresh start. But what would it cure? There would be a new crop of women to choose from and once again, my identity would be the same: the dutiful wife with a straying husband. Nothing but his location would change. My hurt would continue to be pierced by his infidelity. Defeated, I embraced complacency and comfort and wrapped myself in the security blanket of my broken marriage vows, hoping for change. Without shame, his sexual sins continued, those I knew about, and those held tightly in private sanctuaries. But what did I expect? I didn't believe in divorce. He didn't believe in marriage. How were we ever compatible?

Chapter Thirty-Six

Scout's Honor

The more I thought about the turmoil I was going through, the more I had to dissect my marital integrity. Carter owed me more than he would ever acknowledge. No one in their right mind, not even me, should have endured the type of love he gave me. For that, he owed me a letter of recommendation for being a good wife, a good mother, a doormat, a secret sharer, a truth hider, and a fool.

I felt I'd earned my merit badge for marital tolerance. My prior self-esteem badges had been tarnished and remained tucked away in the recesses of my mind, like the pretty lingerie I wore the last time I felt like I mattered to my husband. I became increasingly aware of the need to memorialize my accomplishment with an oath reminiscent of the one I recited while donning my scout uniform. But, instead of raising my right hand, I raised my left hand, extended my middle finger, and recited my version of an oath more appropriate for victimized wives and other women like me.

At the expense of my dignity, I will do my duty to protect my lifestyle and the fantasy I've created.

I will redact portions of my wedding vows to conform to my current shame.

I will dismiss any hints of courage and the echoes of my family's concerns.

I will disregard the lessons taught by my mother and the fears expressed by my father.

I will cover all bruises, black eyes, and broken spirits.

I will never allow tears or sorrow to be displayed on my face.

I will be the shining example of submission for my daughter and desperation for my son.

I will look lovingly into his eyes when he determines it's necessary.

I will perform my conjugal duties as dictated by my mate.

I will utter scripted sounds of imaginary passion.

I will suppress the urge to gag when our tongues touch.

I will squeeze my eyes shut from disgust and not passion.

I will dare my trapped tears to betray me from behind closed eyes.

I will repeat my performance until he no longer finds me worthy.

I will honor my commitment until he no longer wants or needs me.

I will do what's necessary to remain in the good graces of a person who doesn't love me, value me or treat me as an equal.

These things I do begrudgingly to maintain my economic status and perpetuate the lies I had been conditioned to believe. This is my pledge and my sacrifice for the status I once thought I needed.

Chapter Thirty-Seven

My Eyes

The more time Eva and I spent together, the more entangled our lives became. But I didn't care. There was a need and hunger inside me to learn more about my husband's love story with her. Over coffee one day, I recounted our conversation from the day we met. She nodded in acknowledgment before I asked, "Eva, what made you ask if my face had ever looked like yours?

She took a sip of her coffee, gathered her thoughts, then responded, "Your eyes. I don't know if you understand the passageway to your soul they provide. They expose pieces of the person you hide behind to keep yourself from falling apart."

I paused and let that sink into my spirit. Carter had branded me with his abuse, and Eva quickly recognized it. She really did see me. I don't think Carter ever acknowledged the depth of destruction his physical and mental abuse caused me. But, what did I let him see? By remaining silent, had I been as culpable as Carter?

Eva continued, "Frailty and apprehension showed through your eyes. Your demeanor reminded me of my mother's after my father passed. He went to work one day and never came home. I saw that same pain and conflict raging behind your eyes. I don't know if you realized how they reflected your inner thoughts."

I was surprised at how observant she was. My mother always told me that she could read me through my eyes. I didn't really believe her until then.

"Grace, after you saw the look of familiarity with his work, I could tell you didn't want to be there. Big Mama always talked about trees being known by the fruit they bear. She always told me that even if you call an apple tree a pecan tree, the harvest will be apples. It was her way of saying that the person you are will always show up, no matter how hard you try to hide it. Your eyes told me your story. I saw parts of myself in your eyes."

My mind traveled back to my conversations with Carter's mother. She talked about leopards and how their spots can't change no matter how you dress them up. Then I recalled my doll with the broken leg and couldn't help but think of my own spots. The childhood conversation I had with my mother echoed in my ears.

"What's the matter with your baby doll, Grace?"

"I broke its leg."

"Do you want me to try to fix it?"

"No, it'll be ok. I'll just cover that broken piece up with her dress."

"Putting clothes to cover the body of a broken doll doesn't make it whole again. It's still broken and will remain that way until you fix it."

"It's ok for now. Nobody will know but me."

For years I'd tried to apply my eight-year-old logic to my adult problems. It didn't work well for either situation. I walked away from that meeting aware that my life was more transparent than I thought. If Eva saw me, so did my family. I was too ashamed to admit what they knew. Hiding the truth never works for very long; it will always come out. You eventually show who you really are, the you that's on display when nobody is looking. In my case, someone was always watching.

After that encounter, the space between Eva and I gradually decreased. It seemed we had so much in common. Somewhere amid revelation and surrender, I found a kindred spirit. Never would I have imagined finding beauty in the soul of someone who was supposed to be my mortal enemy. Because of her, I could release some of the angst that had been sitting in my gut since the first faceless person shattered my illusions of forever. Once I'd become jaded, I'd never considered their plight. As Eva demonstrated, some of them, and even me, had been trapped by Carter's deception.

Between us, currents of strength and deep respect flowed. Meeting Eva and her baby was one of the most crushing and joyous moments I'd experienced in a while. She didn't understand the impact she had on my life. The scabs of isolation fell away and exposed my soul to someone who was practically a stranger. Eva became my icon of hope. I admired her strength and fight, wrapped in courage and warmth. Before meeting her, I forgot who I could be once I'd forgotten who I was. That person vanished inside Carter's black hole of control, but I believed Eva's example could guide me to recover pieces of the person I'd lost years ago.

From the outside looking in, the dynamics between us were odd. But I felt differently. The cross-pollination of our lives and experiences drew us closer. We shared two men living in one body. I would never know how many other men roamed inside his head but was sure all of them were the same wounded person who punished those brave enough to contradict his illusion of manhood. We both saw who he was; only one of us was brave enough to use our voice. Eva became the public face of my darkness and the voice that had been stuck in my throat for so long. We were bonded by the confluence of our pain and heartache. Society's myopic views about relationships required adjustments for it to understand our perspective. The ugly things we

144

shared would forever connect us and the collective beauty that existed in our children would bond us beyond the limits of our creation. Our common humanity transcended all preconceived notions and propelled our hearts to seek the highest form of admiration. She for me. Me for Joy. Us for our children.

Chapter Thirty-Eight

My Affair

After all the years of Carter's abuse, at no time had I developed an interest in an extramarital relationship with anyone until I met Eva. I was intimately involved in an emotional affair with my husband's mistress. I had to cultivate our liaison in secret. She was becoming the girlfriend I always needed. I felt I could confide in her without judgment. We shared some of the same secrets, and we understood the gentle, romantic parts of my husband. We both divulged things that resulted in raised eyebrows and coy smiles. We were the proverbial odd couple. It had all the earmarks of something abnormal.

No one would ever imagine we'd find a way to be together. It seemed strange, even to me. I wondered if my fascination with her was voyeuristic or at a minimum, selfish, and less than honest. Based on the foundation of our bond, how could it not be? Naturally, I wanted to know about her. I wanted a glimpse into their relationship to see if he treated her better than he treated me. That I wasn't jealous was the joke I kept telling myself. I tried to tell myself that my interest was purely from a non-emotional viewpoint. That wasn't exactly true either. My emotions were the reason I picked up the phone and called her initially and why I kept spending more time with her.

I questioned if what we shared was healthy or if our motives seemed pure. Were we torturing each other because of the different relationship we had with my husband? Why couldn't we hate each other? I was supposed to hate her for what she did to my family, and she was supposed to despise me for begging for my husband's freedom. I wondered if she thought any of this was real or if it was contrived to gain insight for my husband's legal team. I kept waiting for her to rebel against my invitations, but she continued to meet with me and discuss our common interests.

We often shared pictures of and talked about our children. When she showed me photos of Joy, I couldn't help but coo over the brightness and beauty that radiated from behind the glossy images of love. I genuinely cared about the well-being of the child. After all, she was my children's sibling. That fact would never change. They shared visible DNA.

Despite all the things we shared, we didn't discuss anything related to the prosecution of my husband. That elephant was always in the room but didn't play a significant role in our relationship. We each were content to look around it when it tried to interject itself into our conversation. We abided by an unwritten truce. If we got too close to that subject, I'd have to become the dutiful wife, and she'd have to become the home-wrecking mistress. Neither of those roles suited us but would never change, no matter how fond we became of each other.

Once my horizon brightened and I gained space and independence; my feelings about many things changed. My mindset on life had shifted drastically from where it started before that emboldened hospital visit. I'd spent many nights since our first meeting comparing how my life differed from hers. I envied her strength, confidence, and honesty. We were both broken but healing different scars. How ironic that the place I never went to for help, became the place where my broken pieces started to reassemble. Eva helped put a cast on my brokenness. I was sent to that hospital on a mission to secure my husband's freedom. Instead, I walked away carrying newfound seeds of freedom for myself. Carter had underestimated the value of human kindness.

As much as I enjoyed our union, I theorized that eventually, I would have to give her up. I didn't want to think about how difficult that would be. I couldn't fathom the ridicule I'd face from everybody, family included, if we were ever found out. Carter and his family would probably say I was consorting with the enemy and call me a traitor. My friends and family would probably call me a fool, and there was no telling what Eva's mother would say with her knife. I didn't care. I kept telling myself to be brave; she was worth it. I needed Eva more than she needed me and more than I wanted to admit. I needed her to save me.

Chapter Thirty-Nine

He Loves Me Not

The more time we spent together, the more our comfort level grew. We were respectful of each other's feelings and never tried to say or do anything that would hurt the other. We steered clear of the elephant that was always seated at our table. As we each got to know parts of the other's experience, I longed to know the Ben that seemed to have cared deeply for Eva. There was one question that had lingered in my throat since our first meeting. I wanted the answer but wasn't sure I could accept her response.

"Eva, did you love him?"

"Maybe, but I can't tell now."

"Why do you say that?"

"Because love is not supposed to hurt. If I say I did, it will hurt you. I think I've done enough of that already."

I tried desperately not to show the emotions that were spinning around in my mind. I hoped the poker face I'd perfected with my husband could betray her as well. It didn't. She saw my pain. Our eyes met, and Eva quickly looked down into the cup of coffee she nervously corralled in her hands. I encouraged her to be honest. I wanted to know the truth.

"I don't know now but I think I could have. The first day I saw Ben in that coffee shop, I was intrigued."

"Let me guess, he bought you an anonymous cup of coffee."

"Yes. How did you know?"

"That's how we met." Leopards and spots. I was sure she wasn't the first of his love interests to experience the coffee shop hustle.

We continued our conversation, and I let her talk for as long as we both felt comfortable.

"That day in the coffee shop, he was so charming. I met him shortly after Big Mama passed and I needed someone to make me feel alive again. I thought he was a gift from her."

"What do you mean?"

Eva painfully recounted the passing of her grandmother and the emotional toll it took on her. I further understood how vulnerable she would've been and how easily she was swept away by Carter's charm.

"What about you, Grace? After everything that's happened, do you still love him?"

"I think so, but don't really know right now." I could tell by the look on Eva's face that the response confused her. I continued, "I was a struggling nursing student when I met him and he took care of me, even before we got married. He paid for my car, my first apartment, gave me money, and always showered me with gifts. He was a good provider, and I was never fearful of being without. The longer we stayed together, that's what love felt like to me. For the most part, he was my childhood fantasy come to life. He checked all my boxes, plus some."

"Grace, please don't tell me you don't know what real love feels like? You have two babies."

I stared at her, too afraid to comment when I thought about the initial motivation behind getting pregnant with my son, CJ. Deep down, I knew it wasn't from deep parental yearnings.

"Grace, have you ever loved someone so much that when you were together, you didn't know where you ended and they began? That you were the only one for each other?"

I nodded in agreement, but my mind shouted, "No."

How odd that I'd never acknowledged that fact. I wondered if that meant I'd never been in love but in competition. I continued to stare at her face and heard her voice, but my mind kept asking me why I'd never loved that fiercely. I had no answer. Maybe I was infatuated by what Carter had instead of who he was. Had I been hypnotized by the shiny trinkets and gifts? Was this the glass my father saw that caused doubt about our getting married? My father saw parts of his Uncle Charles in Carter. Not until the mask was pulled away from his face did I see the person my father warned me about. By then, it was too late.

I finally responded to Eva's question and said, "I don't know. I think that I could have. "What about you?"

Without hesitation, Eva said, "I definitely know what love is. The love of my life was Adam. I loved him hard and deep. When he no longer wanted me, it crushed my soul. I couldn't find my center once he removed himself from my life. I didn't know who I was without Adam."

I experienced the opposite. I didn't know who I was with Carter. I lost part of myself when I discovered I wasn't enough for him not to embrace infidelity.

"I tried to find the love I had for Adam with my body and not my heart. I was wallowing through life, searching for relief that couldn't be found in the physical realm. Those were times I wish I could take back."

"How long did it take you to get over Adam."

"Years. Big Mama told me I had to forgive him, or I would be stuck in a spin cycle of strange beds. I had to let him go. When I did, I was free."

While I internalized how she recovered from heartbreak, she said, "Believe it or not, I've already forgiven Ben. I can't say the same thing for my mother. It's gonna take some time for her, but it gets easier each time she holds Joy." Eva gently placed her hand on mine and said, "You'll know when it's time."

151

I didn't know if I believed her. He almost killed her and her baby. I hadn't forgiven him for that yet. How could she?

Chapter Forty

Cornered

At our last outing, Eva talked about being free. I didn't know what that felt like. I'd been too constrained by the boundaries of what pleased Carter to understand how anyone else lived. Even while he sat in jail, the parallel effects of the physical and mental imprisonment I'd endured kept me bound. It was hard to think of my life beyond the restrictive borders of the invisible fence that surrounded me. I was still afraid to stray too far beyond his conditioning. I didn't want to get used to a new way of living and thinking, only to have it ripped away when Carter came home. But I could feel parts of the fence slowly coming down. As it got lower, I began to consider taking steps toward the freedom that existed beyond his reach.

As I drove to meet Eva, I thought about how the enlacement of our past would forever bind us. When I walked into the restaurant, Eva was already there with Joy. The tremors of an earthquake radiated through me until I sat down at the table. In the span of time it took to walk from the door to the table, my heart broke several times. Seeing Joy was painful, but those feelings were overpowered by the love and admiration that glistened in the eyes of a new mother. After Eva explained her mother's unavailability, I was relieved. I didn't want to feel exploited by having my husband's child flaunted in my face. I couldn't help but think how Carter would feel if he could see me with Eva and his other daughter.

I couldn't fight the urge to touch her. She looked so different from the tiny being who'd ruptured my soul a few months earlier. When I reached over and pinched her cheek, I suppressed the impulse to draw my hand back as if my fingertips had touched a hot coil. I'd touched one of my husband's children that didn't belong to me. I quietly prayed for strength. Eva looked surprised when I asked if I could hold her. Something inside me stirred as I held Joy in my arms. Her innocence radiated through her eyes as she returned my gaze with no agenda. I was immediately filled with peace. Holding her was setting me free.

As Joy slept, our conversation was light until we started to talk about children.

"Grace, how are your children coping with all that's going on with their father? I'm sure they have a lot of questions, especially since he's not home."

I was almost embarrassed when I said, "They've been with my parents since Carter's arrest. I'm trying to keep them away from as much of this as possible. I wanted them to have more than I could give them while things were getting sorted out. I never thought it would take this long."

"Grace, one thing Big Mama taught me was that children need their mother. Your children need to hear the truth from you before their minds become polluted with someone else's version of their family's story. Don't let them have to guess about the love you have for them. Show them by being there. They don't need to have both parents ripped from their lives. Trust me, I know."

"How so?"

"After my father died, my mother took me to live with my grandparents. I didn't see her for years. I loved them, but they weren't my mother. In my mind, she abandoned me when I needed her the most. Although she meant well, nothing was the same between us for a long time after that."

"I do spend time with them but probably not as much as I should. They have a routine where they are. Right now, they need the stability I can't give them."

"I understand, but as my Big Mama used to say, "Mothering ain't no part-time job. Whether you feel like it or not, your children are counting on you. Children don't care about routines or motives. They care about what they're missing from their parents. And right now, you're the only one they have."

I looked at her and said, "Have you been talking to my mother behind my back?"

After we both laughed, she said, "No, I'm speaking to you from experience. Grace, your children need you. I know what it's like to feel unwanted by your mother. I wouldn't wish that on anybody. It took me a long time to get over that hurt. I wasted too many years that I can't get back, festering in anger."

After I thought about the similar words that had been expressed by both Eva and my mother, I said, "Isn't it funny how our parents can see around corners we haven't gotten to yet? I never considered my absence through the eyes of my children."

"I get it. The way Big Mama explained it to me was that when you flip a coin, the side that's facing down never gets looked at. The important side is the one we can see. Right now, they can see you, not your husband."

As we got up to leave, Eva picked up Joy and said, "Grace, go get your babies. They need you now, more than ever."

"Just think, we'll have to come up with sayings like that in a few years. It will be one more thing they won't want to hear from us old people."

Chapter Forty-One

Quiet Mouse

Each time I met with Eva, I left with some nuance of her authenticity and wisdom. At one of our meetings, she said, "Grace, don't you think it's time to love yourself? If you don't, who will?"

It disturbed me that she could see me so clearly. It was written all over me that I didn't really know what real love looked, felt, or acted like. The pain I endured from feeling unloved altered me. Every day, I hoped for more but expected less. I wondered when I would fall in love with myself and stop waiting for my husband to love the person I was. I felt like a lonely star. Even though I occupied a place high in the heavens, it didn't protect me from being overlooked in search of other constellations. I was constantly overshadowed by the stars around me. I never felt bright enough to be singled out and named as a symbol of forever. I was destined to be ordinary, taking up space until I slowly burned out while no one noticed.

Scenes that spanned from our wedding day until it devolved down to our abridged form of marriage, flashed through my mind. I saw how doing nothing wasn't free. It cost me everything, my dignity, my self-worth, and at times, I feared, my life. Like a spectator, I sat by and watched my marriage fall apart in slow motion. I was powerless to stop the infidelity bus from running over me time and time again. I got tired of getting hit by it. I made it easy for the bus. I laid down and became part of the pavement, barely a notice-able speed bump. I often wondered how my life would've been had I not stayed with Carter. I'd given up so much and appeared to have gotten so little of the happiness quotient I figured up in my head. No matter how hard I tried, I couldn't love him out of the infidelity. I wasn't enough.

Our ruptured relationship staggered along for years, be-ing continually weighted down by unsafe secrets that longed to shout out their displeasure with cries of relief. Our hearts were not together. Sad to say that they never were. In theory, maybe, but not in practice. An erosion of confidence in our marriage began with his first indiscretion. After it started again, the snowball effect took over and rolled faster and faster, like a bowling ball down the aisle of our marriage. I toppled over once the weight of his actions hit me in the heart. Once it went straight through me, it never stopped. It took on a life of its own. The locusts of his cruelty ate away at my self-esteem until all that was left was an empty shell. No harvest was possible.

His infidelity cost him nothing while I continued to pay the price. I was always haunted by the ghosts of affairs past. To amuse myself, I made up a myriad of diseases Carter could become inflicted with. Because of the number of sweet treats he kept consuming outside the boundaries of our marriage, I hoped he would develop a case of adulterous diabetes. I often wondered how he avoided getting tooth decay. Neuropathy of the penis sounded like a good one. With the numbness, cramps, and weakness he would suffer, straying wouldn't be so appealing. Maybe a case of genital nausea would be just punishment for his overindulgent ap-petite for variety. He'd constantly been over-eating for quite a while. As much as those quirky notions entertained me, the underlying issue crushed me. I felt obsolete.

Even when I knew the love was over, I stayed. I didn't know how to break away from the bad and keep the good. We no longer had a closeness or bond that existed between soulmates. Once our emotional intimacy stopped being cultivated, it died on the vine. The evident reality of my marriage became irrelevant once I decided to keep fighting. I was drowning in three feet of water but was too foolish to stand up. I wanted to stay in there, fight against the current, and learn to swim. What I realized was that swimming wasn't the only option. It was just the one I focused on. After a while, I got used to the sadness and found ways to divert my pain and loneliness with numbered plastic and gift bags. Those temporary distractions helped interrupt my pain auras and allowed me to have brief moments of contentment. I'd spent so much time running and reaching, trying to fill my arms with what my heart lacked, that I forgot the beauty of being quiet and still. I hadn't experienced that type of silence in a while. But once I yielded to the stillness, I knew I'd had enough. I was becoming more powerful than I'd ever been before.

Now, on the brink of his trial, whose outcome I deemed a foregone conclusion, decisions would be made for me that I wouldn't have the option to change. It would be out of my hands. I always said I wanted to see my vows through to the end. Mission accomplished.

Chapter Forty-Two

Mad Day

The pursuit of justice churned slowly. I watched the seasons change outside my window. Some aspects of my life stood still while others marched forward. The day after his arrest, I stared out the window at fallen leaves caught in the whirlwind effect of the autumn wind. They spun in harmony until gravity dispersed them into overlapping layers of color. Virgin snow gathered on bushes and trees that were once filled with leaves and flowers, making them appear to have been replaced with cotton. Barren trees regained their foliage as once-hardened earth pushed forth a dormant array of color. Flowers bloomed as bees welcomed the fragrant source of nectar while a rainbow of birds sang territorial melodies. Days became longer and warmer, causing clothing to become thinner and shorter. The sounds of bodies splashing in swimming pools filled the days, while the array of light from fireworks dotted the night sky. Sadly, the fallen leaves returned while I continued to wait.

The waiting would be over soon. The trial started in a week. My contribution to his defense was to provide the wardrobe. As I walked through his closet, I let my hand wander over the sleeves of his suits, each one allowing the others to take its turn at being selected. The fabric of the blue pinstripe I chose seemed to caress my arm as it took its place of honor. I closed my eyes and felt the arms of the suit magically surround me in an embrace as I danced in silence with my husband. When I opened my eyes to look at his face, it slipped out of my grasp and landed on the floor. I picked it up, selected the final pieces, and turned off the light. I couldn't shut off my emotions as easily. I allowed my mind to drift, stopping at a time when I thought we had it all. We were like two birds perched high on a wire, sharing secrets no one else could hear, using a language only we understood. I lingered there for as long as I could fight off our current reality.

When I laid his clothes on the bed, more memories flooded my mind. I felt the brush of his fingers against my cheek and the back of his neck against the inside of my wrist as the softness of his lips covered mine. I remembered the smacking sounds of our last kiss, the minty smell of his breath, the faint smell of lip balm, and the fragrant trail of his cologne drifting up my nose. Smitten eyes remained glued to him as I watched him walk across the room and through the double doors. I heard the clicking sound of the closing door before I sank back into the scene of the passion we just shared. Little did I know those would be the last sounds we'd share in the bowels of our sanctuary before our lives changed forever.

The storm brewing inside my soul caused the internal turmoil to manifest trickling rain streaks from my eyes. I'd gone from being madly in love to just plain mad. How could this be my life? I'd asked myself that same question over the last few months. The ground beneath me shifted and toppled over my unstable life like the blocks in a Jenga game. Unlike the game, our lives wouldn't survive the fall. Too many pieces were broken and scattered to ever be perfectly stacked up again. Nothing would ever be the same.

The anger of a thousand days began to make its way to the surface. I couldn't hold back what needed to be released. I had to let out my feelings. I screamed as loud and as long as my throat and lungs would allow. The heavy breathing and exhaustion, along with the tiny beads of perspiration, mimicked the aftermath of intense conjugal satisfaction. I needed that release and knew I would feel better if I repeatedly partook of the newfound pleasure until my throat and body could no longer tolerate the self-love affair. When my throat no longer allowed sounds to escape, I rolled over, pulled the covers up to my neck, and let exhaustion put me to sleep.

I felt refreshed the next morning, determined not to let anger continue to consume me. Days of wallowing in hurt and anger showed in my surroundings. As much as I wanted to, I couldn't ignore the counter full of take-out containers, the sink full of dirty dishes, or two weeks' worth of dirty laundry. While my hands roamed through the laundry baskets, thoughts of my disjointed life swirled around in my head. How easy it would be to throw everything in the washer and accept what came out. I didn't care if the whites stayed white or soaked up the cast-offs of vibrant colors until it was a tie-dyed mess. I didn't care if anything would be worth keeping.

My life was being imitated by a pile of dirty laundry. I'd been thrown into the middle of Carter's spin cycle of lies and was left with the changes brought about by a whirlwind of disturbing revelations. I didn't want to keep any of it. I wished I could bag up all my problems and drop them off at the Goodwill. But I knew I had to stay there and sort through the fragmented pieces of my life and decide what needed to be folded and put away and what needed to be washed again. Some pieces were so soiled that the overpowering smell of Clorox bleach or the fragrant aroma of Downy couldn't make them tolerable. I knew it would be a long time before I would be able to breathe deeply without gagging on regret. After one load was finished, I called Eva. The others could wait.

Chapter Forty-Three

My Damascus Road

Over our many outings, Eva shared snippets of her relationship with Carter. I often wondered what he was like with her. Sometimes when details were confided, I became jealous of the stolen affection gifted to someone who never knew the real name of the man she thought she loved. Other times, we were kindred spirits of suffering. When she talked about her decision to keep the baby over Carter's objections, I understood the depth of his anger and the reason for his brutal attack. His lies and his lack of control over Eva's maternal decision pushed him over the edge. His public persona was in jeopardy. I remembered the taste of the gun in my mouth after I caused the police to show up at our door. We'd both learned the hard way that no one messed with his image.

The weekend before the trial, Eva decided to give me access to something she understood I needed but would never vocalize. She fumbled in her handbag, pulled out a set of keys, and placed one of them on the table. As she moved it in my direction, she gave me the address of her truth. Before she got up to leave, she placed her hand over mine and said, "When you're ready."

My fingertips refused to touch the key; avoiding it like it was toxic and could singe my skin. I wondered if its weight would require both hands to lift it. To my surprise, it only took two fingers to place the key in my purse. Accepting her offering would change everything. It would uncover things I'd often wondered about Carter and the places that drew him away from me. I couldn't resist the opportunity to see where they shared a normal existence and conceived their love child, the place where he was so many nights when I needed him. No doubt their love nest was his conference destination, missed flight, rescheduled meeting, demanding client, and, eventually, his crime scene.

Commonplace was how everything looked on my Damascus road. It was the same address from Carter's computer beside Eva's name. Even the for-sale sign was welcoming. Although the aesthetics of the neighborhood were welcoming, my focus was on getting a chance to pull the curtain back further on that edition of Carter's infidelity. The person Eva got to know as Ben was waiting to be revealed. Thinking of how he felt each time he parked his car in her driveway, pampered her with gifts and expressions of affection, caused me to question how I measured up to the last woman he chose over his family.

The façade of the building looked as ordinary as my marriage felt. Neither felt special. How much more insignificant would I feel standing inside the space my husband shared with Eva? Secrets meant to be hidden forever were waiting to be extracted. I expected to detect whiffs of the familiar scent of his cologne and be engulfed by the lingering smell of flowers that undoubtedly filled her apartment as my ears burned from echoes of laughter, moans of passion, good-bye kisses at the door, and giggles before a playful touch on the nose. My shoulders slumped over from the weight of the events of the last few months. I was sinking into the earth each time I picked one foot up and prepared to wade deeper into the ocean of lies and selfishness that jeopardized our family.

The apartment was pristine, fresh, and empty. It held no sign of the brutality that caused its vacancy. I'd read the police report and viewed photos of the crime scene with

Carter and his attorney. Gone was the trail of blood and determination that started and ended after the assault. I looked at the distance and marveled at her strength and will to preserve not only her life but the life of her child. A rebel tear demanded its presence be added to the history of the floor. I caught the others that sought to follow its lead.

My eyes immediately found the spot that marked his territorial barrage of anger against Eva. My emotions were being battered and tossed around like rag dolls. Screams, begging, promises of repentance, and the crashing sounds of unanchored objects filled the room. Spatters of blood and mucous tattooed the floors and walls. Uncontrollable rage spewed through his pores as forceful words demanded submission. Bulging eyes showed no remorse while strong hands stole badly needed air from burning lungs. Sighs of relief, followed by coughing and tears, filled the room when the door slammed behind him. I flinched from the sound and realized I wasn't home but was still inside Eva's apartment. Everything felt so familiar. No matter the location, Carter acted the same. Eva had lived my truth; we shared so many physical and emotional scars.

I wandered deeper into their love nest. The hallway was short, but the ten steps from the living room to the bedroom felt like twenty. The sterile setting relieved some avenues of tension but fostered more hurt and twinges of jealousy. I saw the impressions left by the bed that marked the spot where he lay with Eva. I imagined how the room was decorated, how often he left the covers tossed, and how he spent mornings in bed with her. It was becoming too much for me. I wanted to run but couldn't. I had to see everything.

Eva's version of how she found out about our marriage replayed in my head as I walked toward the bathroom. She could've overheard the entire conversation from where I stood. And knowing Carter, he would've blocked out everything while he talked to our daughter, Taylor. I tried to imagine Eva's confusion the moment she heard Carter talking about our anniversary. She was probably as shocked as I was the first time I got a call from another woman. I understood her sense of betrayal, but she didn't understand that the person on the other end of the line was someone who had the right to be an intruder on her happiness. One conversation produced different acts of disruption. My joy, her pain.

I was still processing everything after leaving the bedroom and remembered the conversation from that night and his calm demeanor the day of the assault. How my husband walked away from this apartment after such a brutal outburst and greeted me the same morning with gentle hugs, a bright smile, and numerous gifts in celebration of our sacred union blew my mind. A chill ran through my body when I wondered if he had blood on his hands that was washed away at our home. A heightened feeling of betrayal engulfed me knowing my anniversary date had been stolen from me. There would never be another marking of our union that could be celebrated without remembering the tragedy that would forever be tied to that day. I was mentally exhausted and ready to go home. When I got to the front door, I paused. Bits and pieces of Eva's version of his final desperate act of aggression rang in my ear. I heard his quickened steps as he moved toward Eva's battered body before I closed my eyes. I didn't want to witness Carter's attempt to abort his own child. I'd seen enough.

I sat in my car and took deep breaths, trying to contain the flood of emotions that followed me from Eva's apartment. My mannequin-like eyes showed no signs of the hurt that saturated my being. They weren't allowed to produce tears. I was beginning to understand the gravity of the artificial life I'd been living. My constant denial of one part of Carter's secret life had been needed more than I could've imagined. It was the lifeblood of my sanity. It was what I needed to survive.

As I was driving away, I noticed the "for sale" sign in the yard had been covered with the word "sold" while I was inside. Maybe someone would be able to breathe life back into the space and fill it once again with happiness. I pulled down the visor and looked to see if "for sale" was stamped on my forehead. I'd sold myself to Carter. It hadn't been a wise investment.

Chapter Forty-Four

Under Oath

The first day of trial was unnerving. I walked into the courtroom, carrying the memories of my visit to the scene of the crime, and sat down beside Carter's mother. By my side should have been all the other women who enjoyed Carter's body and monetary support over the years. Here was their chance to replace me and let others know of their entanglement with my husband. They could show the world how much he meant to them. Here was their chance to profess their gratitude for the trips, houses, clothes, jewelry, and time their bodies had paid for. Now was their chance to publicly feel what it was like to be Mrs. Carter Mann. Clearly, suffering through the court hearings wasn't a perk that interested them. They were content to leave that task up to me. And after his dark side was exposed to the world, I was sure his name was deleted so quickly by his female "friends" that the alphabet laughed. I was sure they thanked God they didn't end up like Eva. He was solely my responsibility now.

After settling in the gallery as the dutiful wife, I looked across the courtroom at Eva and her mother. A faint smile of acknowledgment from Eva was contrasted by her mother's threatening eyes. Those same eyes that watched me that day in the hospital still said her knife was in her purse. I quickly turned away and engaged in pleasant banter with my mother-in-law. She'd always been at every court procedure and showed support for Carter from the beginning of his ordeal. She didn't care if he was innocent or guilty, he was her son. The way she put it was, "Never put someone outside during a storm." I agreed. I'd vowed for better or for worse and he was still my husband.

From the moment I entered the courtroom, it felt like every eye was on me. I was being watched like the tally indicator on the Jerry Lewis telethon. Repeated stares and whispers caused me to crave invisibility. Curious eyes filled with conjecture and innuendo surrounded me and searched for understanding. I knew what it felt like to be a guppy inside a fishbowl. I wanted everyone to look away from me when their intrusive eyes searched for signs of his abuse. I wondered how many of those eyes were filled with sympathy and quiet recognition. I was sure some of those who silently judged me had walked several miles in my shoes.

Common sense told everyone Eva was not his first victim. Undoubtedly, he'd honed his skills with me. Questions were entertained about how someone who looked like me could have withstood the double whammy of infidelity and abuse. I was probably being called every adjective of weakness they could think of and every version of a fool in the dictionary. But those were Carter's sins, not mine. Why was I being judged? I defended myself by giving them nothing interesting to look at. Beneath the façade created by attitude, attire, and makeup, no one could see the stress cracks in my mask of composure. I was falling apart on the inside, while my outside presented calmness. I was proud of my mastery of false face. Years of practice prepared me for that moment.

I wasn't prepared for the onslaught of emotions that constantly cascaded around me. Each time a new photo of the assault was presented, the gallery echoed in unison with sounds of shock and whispers. I had to look away from those images. I'd never encountered such gruesome views of the handiwork of my husband. I'd been too afraid to record any of myself for fear of retaliation and more severe punishment. I substituted my face on the pictures of Carter's brutality against Eva. Both of our bodies were tattooed with the blueprints of his anger.

The enlarged pictures the prosecutor displayed spooked me. The skeletons in my closet rattled, even though it wasn't Halloween. Most of the time, I showed no emotion, as if my face had been overly treated with Botox. Other times, the memories of assaults that resurrected in familiar places on my body caused me to wince. The marks on Eva's neck caused me to slowly grab the front of mine as if Carter's forceful fingers were locked around my neck, separating my lungs from the air. I struggled to take a deep breath and coughed after barely escaping suffocation. My exterior remained calm but, on the inside, my screams were so loud I barely heard the gavel signal the end of the morning session.

After the midday recess, Eva was called to testify. I braced myself for a sympathetic recounting of his abuse chronicles. We exchanged fleeting glances as she made her way to the witness stand. The key to her apartment was still in my purse. Because of the relationship we'd built, apologizing to her for sitting in support of my husband seemed warranted. Although we wouldn't judge each other for the roles we had to play, fulfilling my obligation still felt inappropriate. Just as Eva was under oath to reveal her truth, my vows were my promise to keep mine hidden. When Carter initially coaxed me into meeting Eva, I thought it could be the best thing for me and our marriage. My instincts were correct, but not for the reasons I'd considered. Learning that my husband was the father of Eva's baby began to loosen the love grip he had on me. Destiny, disguised as curiosity, guided me to the nursery window. Devastation led to the admiration of an enemy who extended comfort in the middle of a war. It was the beginning of the end of my doing nothing about our marital secrets and lies. That was when my life changed.

When Eva sat down in the witness chair, my mother-in-law placed her hand on mine and kept it there throughout her testimony. I was grateful. Her hand probably kept me from taking my designer shoe off, beating Carter in the back of the head with it, and claiming self-defense. Eva testified openly and honestly about her affair with my husband. Even though we'd spoken candidly about their history, hearing the details in open court still wounded me. The things I wanted to keep hidden from the world were on public display. Nothing was private anymore. The dark side of our lives became the secret everybody knew. An encapsulated version of a horror I never wanted to admit would be archived forever. My efforts had been in vain.

Chapter 45

Lesson From the Storm

"From the WRPE news desk, the trial of prominent business-man Carter Mann got underway today. The prosecution laid the foundation for a guilty verdict via graphic photos, evidence, and shocking testimony from the victim. The trial is set to resume on Monday. We will continue to provide updates as the trial progresses. Stay tuned to WRPE, your information station."

The prosecution rested its case shortly after the midday recess, and the court dismissed early. On Monday, Carter's attorney would present his defense. It was Friday and spending the entire weekend with CJ and Taylor would help me recover from the rigors of court. After talking with Eva about her separation story, I decided to bring my children back home where they belonged. Hearing a child's perspective opened my eyes to what they were going through. My parents were sad for them to leave but understood the need for us to live as a family again. I still hadn't told them about their sister. I'd know when it was the right time.

When I stopped to pick up the children, my sister had already consented to a sleep-over at her house. She'd heard the news update and decided to give me a break for the evening. After picking up dinner, my last stop was the liquor store for a nice bottle of wine. I got home before the early evening thunderstorms began. Although it felt good to be home alone, the house was too quiet. It needed to be filled with good noise. I couldn't decide between watching a movie or listening to music. Either would overtake the sights and sounds of the day. I turned the television volume up and put on my favorite music. It seemed appropriate to have such dueling distractions, given the tone of the day and the weather. The impending storm reminded me of the chaos swirling around my life. Hopefully, both the storm and the chaos would end quickly.

My mind ached for an escape from anything that had to do with the trial. With a glass of wine in my hand, I kicked off my shoes and danced around in circles, focusing on the bass sounds of the music. For those bars of music, I felt alive and free, so far removed from my courtroom performance requirements. Through every session, I quieted my own demons and tried to remain emotionless, while appearing to look supportive of my husband. The sounds of gavels banging, chairs moving from the standing up and sitting down of attorneys, and the hushed sounds of people who watched the tragic consequences of our lives for entertainment, were so far away.

My thoughts were as restless as the weather and hindered my attempt at mental separation. The weatherman was accurate about the thunderstorm that became a party-crasher. Without warning, my sounds of escape were replaced by the loudest clap of thunder I'd ever heard. Voices from the radio and television stopped mid-sentence after the power to the house was lost. The substitute companions I'd created were gone. Darkness and a deafening silence encircled me. Lightening illuminated my surroundings in flickering bursts of white. My plans had suddenly been altered by events over which I had no control. My life was being portrayed by nature.

The angry wind howled outside the window and moved debris around at its whim. Displaced leaves and twigs landed against the panes and settled in their new location. The flashes of light enabled me to find the candles in the kitchen drawer and the wine. Together, we'd wait out the storm. During the wait, the effects of the wine caused me to go from sitting on the couch, to leaning on a pillow, to fully stretched out. My heavy eyes focused on the flickering candlelight until it multiplied into points of light too numerous to count. I shielded them from the brightness.

Thousands of fireflies, casting a haunting glow, surrounded me when I uncovered my eyes. As long as I could remember, I always loved fireflies. When I passed them on the road to my house, I fought the urge to turn off the headlights and let their fluorescent glow compete for loveliness with the brightness of the night stars. The pulsating lights of the colony followed their own rhythm like a silent array of firecrackers. My eyes were transfixed on the magical gift of nature. Without hesitation, I followed them deeper and deeper into the unknown as they moved faster and faster away from me. Even though I ran, I couldn't catch them. They always remained just beyond my grasp. It became evident that I'd never get what I wanted. I'd chased them long enough. I sat down to rest and watched the glob of light move further and further away.

When I looked around at the unfamiliar scenery, I realized I was lost. I'd been so distracted by following the light that I didn't know where I was. I was stuck in a place where it was too dark to go back or move forward. I wondered how I'd ever find my way back to where I belonged. I felt so foolish. I'd chosen to go down a dark path to nowhere that left me abandoned and alone with no clear direction in sight.

I'd never considered the consequences of chasing the unattainable. How could I find my way back? If I yelled for help, who would hear me or consider coming to my rescue? I bowed my head and prayed for a miracle. When I looked up, the glow of light returned, stopped, and hovered above me. Its beauty was mesmerizing. I wanted to touch the swarming mass and experience part of the magic that drew me in. As I extended my hand up toward the glow, from somewhere in the darkness, I heard my name. It startled me. Maybe I hadn't been lost and alone.

"Hello. Is anybody there? I'm lost."

"Is that you, Grace?"

"Who's asking?"

"An old friend."

"Who are you?"

"You don't recognize my voice?

"No."

"How sad."

"What do you mean?"

"I am You."

"Me?"

"Yes. The real you. We're soulmates. Even though I've been neglected for a few years, I'm still here."

I began to question everything. It wasn't me. How could it be? I was there. That voice came from somewhere I couldn't see.

"You don't know me or what I need."

"I've always known you. You don't know yourself."

"Tell me something about myself that I don't already know."

"That you are strong. That you deserve better. That you need love."

"I already have love. I'm married. I have a husband. I'm happy with my life."

"At least two of those facts are correct. Love and happiness are missing. "

"I deserve to stay married, and I deserve to be happy."

"Who doesn't? But have you found that happiness yet? Has your husband acted like he was married?"

"No. But once the trial is behind us, he says we will have a chance to start over."

"Why do you believe that?"

"Because I love him and I don't want to give up on my vows."

"Vows are just words. It's the following through with the commitment that counts."

"Stop talking to me. You don't understand."

"Neither do you."

I became silent. I wasn't ready to consider that someone else knew me better than I knew myself. If that was correct, I could get answers to questions that plagued me for years.

"Why are all these bad things happening to me?"

"You know why."

"I've been a good wife to him. I don't deserve this."

"You think you're too good for hard times."

"No, but I feel so betrayed."

"You should. How do you think I felt all these years that I watched you settle for less than who you are at the hands of a man who should love you? Why couldn't you walk away?"

"I needed him."

"Not more than you needed yourself."

"I don't know myself anymore."

"I'm right here, Grace. I never left you."

"You never left me?"

"No, and I never will."

"What do I do now?"

"Rest. You have to prepare for the fight of your life. In order to do that, you have to be yourself again."

I was too tired and confused to argue. All I could do was sob into my hands.

"Go ahead and cry, Grace. Leave as many tears as you can produce. They are yours to give. Let them help cleanse your soul."

As the glow began to vanish, I looked up into the dark sky as drops of rain began to fall. Each droplet contained a tiny prism of light seeking its own destination. I tilted my head back and allowed the volume of the sky's tears to camouflage mine. The coolness of the drops connected with my face and helped soothe the heat my tears created. The intensity of the raindrops increased, drenching my clothing and hair. I pulled my knees to my chest, lowered my head, and waited for the rain to stop.

It didn't stop. The water was pouring on my head so rapidly that I couldn't catch my breath. The heaviness of the steady flow took my breath away. Each half lung full of air came at the expense of fearing I would drown. I needed to move out of that spot. I tried to open my eyes to get my bearings, but I couldn't focus. In an attempt to keep the flow of water at bay, my hands functioned like windshield wipers. When my arms got tired, I wanted to give up, but was afraid of the consequences I'd face. I couldn't tell where all the water was coming from or how to escape from it. The fear of drowning kept me from looking up. I fought harder to keep myself alive. My arms burned from fatigue. "Please, God, help me," I pleaded. "I don't want to die. I don't want to leave my children!"

My body jerked, releasing me from the terror of my nightmare. When I opened my eyes to darkness, my pupils struggled to adjust to the surroundings. The sights and sounds from my dream swirled around in my head. Everything seemed so real. I touched my hair and clothes. They were still dry. It took a minute to realize I wasn't lost deep in the woods; I was in the same spot where I laid earlier. Still, no power, but the storm had passed. It was just me, the house, and my wine-altered thoughts. No more wine. Me and the candle headed for the bedroom.

The mirror reflected enough light from the candle for me to find my pajamas. When I sat down on the bed, I saw a light outside the window. For a moment, I thought the power had been restored in parts of the neighborhood. The light blinked. I smiled when the lone firefly cast its brilliance against a sea of darkness. I thought about that dream and the message delivered to me by the voice in the fireflies. I'd been reminded of who I was and that I needed to start fighting for myself. Sometimes, the things we chase after the most aren't worth the effort. I couldn't continue to exist in artificial luxury at the expense of my dignity. I could no longer hold on to the fantasy of a happy marriage. Doing so only kept me wandering around lost. It was time to move forward.

Chapter Forty-Six

Uprooted Trees

The storm took a toll on nature that night. Somewhere between the loud clapping sound of thunder and the powerful gusts of winds, my landscape changed. A massive tree lay sprawled on the ground with its roots exposed. I didn't realize how fragile something of that stature could be. An exaggerated version of winds that gently kissed my face and caressed my hair days earlier had toppled it over. The relentless battering over an extended period of time finally exploited its weakest point. It became obvious that its plight mirrored the current status of my life. I'd faced strong mental headwinds and knew what it felt like to fall when it appeared you were anchored for life.

I began to compare other aspects of my life to that of the tree. My life had been exposed in a manner that demonstrated the lack of stability at the base of our marriage. It showed the dirt that clung to our existence and ran deep into the fissures of our character. Mud seeped through my pores when I was no longer able to keep inside the mixture of tears, submission, and shame. I empathized with the tree. How could something that had taken so long to grow, end up as kindling because of a traumatic event? The tree couldn't go back into the ground to once again reach toward the heavens. It was too damaged. It appeared to be destined for a sole agonizing demise. Such was the condition of my life. It was falling down around me, and I was powerless in its wake. I couldn't deny the unstableness of my marriage or go back to its beginning. Too many lifetimes had occurred since my heartfelt "I do." Too many horrors had been imposed and shamefully forgotten. I was forced to acknowledge that everyone knew some of the secrets I sacrificed my dignity to protect. I had no choice but to surrender. Just like the tree, I was slowly dying. At least the tree's death would be quick.

Over the next two weeks, I watched the tree slowly succumb to nature's reclamation process. The dark dirt that once surrounded the root ball became lighter from lack of moisture. The converted consistency would soon float into the atmosphere and once again find its way back to mother earth. Each time I passed by, I glanced at the leaves to gauge the storm victim's demise. To my surprise, the tree's slightly wilted leaves remained green. The tree, although damaged, had enough life left to continue living.

One day I stood by the window and stared at the tree, marveling at the beauty of its transformation. I watched as the chirping birds cheerfully hopped from limb to limb, and the squirrel's tails floated effortlessly above the tree's trunk. To them, it appeared the tree's value hadn't changed. Even though it was downed, it still provided gifts of relief in its current state. It was forced to become another version of itself. Whether standing tall or sprawling on the grass, the life it had left still mattered.

I began to see my life reflected in the uprooted tree. It showed me that as long as I had life's breath in my body, there was hope. The power in what remained extended beyond the boundaries of what I could imagine. I needed to work on strengthening the roots of what I had, stop worrying about what I didn't have, and be grateful for the opportunities that lay ahead. The usable pieces of my life would be replanted in soil ready to receive the gifts. My soul was overflowing with peace. A new season was on the horizon.

Chapter Forty-Seven

Turning Point

A more refined version of myself awaited me once I shed my old skin. I had to let go of so much of my fakeness to make room for a new life. Everyone already recognized the lies. The flashing scenes of our time together played over and over in my mind. I couldn't purge the insane thoughts of failure. The emotional crutch I leaned on gave way, and I fell headfirst into the reality and truth of my existence. I had to sit still and allow the transformation to occur. I'd buried my feelings for so many years that I'd almost forgotten what it was like to be my authentic self. I was a whole, broken woman, badly in need of the healing that occurs with love and time. Those broken pieces would form a mosaic that wouldn't remind me of all the things I forfeited, but of the things that were possible.

During the trial, my vision about our marriage became clear. I'd been fitted with the same reality glasses that had been worn by various scorned and battered predecessors. Letters of the eye chart illuminated to spell out exactly what he was. EVIL. Being away from Carter and spending time with Eva, emphasized how much damage I'd allowed him to cause. When I unpacked the bags of my marriage and looked at the contents, I was disgustingly aware of my lack of self-esteem. The corrective lenses I used to see Carter, worked on me as well. They made me see beyond my mask and really look deep inside myself. I saw the aftermath of the marital hunger and neglect I'd endured for far too long. My soul was barely alive and needed to be revived. But that had to start with me. He didn't know how to love me, and I'd forgotten what it felt like to love myself. Gradually over time, the way an icicle succumbs to the unrelenting effects of the sun, I'd lost Grace.

At my inflection point, I had to decide who and what I wanted to be. I couldn't live backward or worry about the things that could've been. There was no point; history can't change. For too long, I'd teetered in limbo in my marriage. I didn't belong anywhere and I was hanging on by a thread, afraid a strong gust of wind would make me choose where I wanted to land. I knew I had to fall forward if I wanted any chance to be more than a subplot in my own life. I had to put myself at the top of my priority list. I'd wasted too much of my time with someone unworthy of my continued devotion.

For the longest time, I'd stopped dreaming or caring about life's possibilities for me. I accepted my fate as my only option and settled in to die a slow, tortured life, filled with the trappings of desperation. I had to learn to dream again. Not only for me but also for our children. They had to see life in me in the midst of all that was falling down around us. They had to learn that getting up after a fall is the only way to move forward. I owed them that much. Odds were the trial wouldn't end in his favor. It was time to envision life post-Carter.

I would never regret loving my husband, once I concluded that it didn't matter to the moon what the sun did. While they had similarities, each was suspended in its own orbit, and their trek across the skies was uniquely independent. Each was as important as the other. Each absence noticed and each return appreciated by the souls they impacted. Such was the pattern of my life. It didn't matter what version of myself I became, Carter was going to be who he was, a man with an angry soul too calloused and hardened to be enriched by genuine love and kindness. He hid behind walls too thick to knock down and too tall to climb. Each time I broke down one barrier, I was disappointed to find another. Each time I reached the top of a wall, beyond the next ridge lay another steep facade. Eventually, my mind and body surrendered. I knew it was time to accept my limits and save what was left of me.

Chapter Forty-Eight

Changing Directions

The last few months of spending time with myself had almost felt too calm. I kept waiting for something more to overtake me. I'd become conditioned for dread like one of Pavlov's dogs. I would wake up with my heart in knots for no reason. I'd been stuck in an infinite loop of sorrow for so long that I didn't know what it was like to adjust to a life without constant turmoil. As a new world unfolded before me, my comfort level increased. There were times when thoughts of failure lurked in my spirit, but I didn't give them a chance to visit their agenda on me. I hadn't failed; I'd just wandered down a path that wasn't the best one for me. Slowly, I was learning to appreciate the person I was getting to know again. I'd only scratched the surface of my substance and intelligence before I met Carter. Once I became involved with him, I settled, plotted, and schemed myself into physical and mental brokenness. Even worse, I'd been too proud and too ashamed to abandon an image of success no one really believed existed but me.

At our core, we all want to be loved and needed; to feel like we matter. Sometimes we take the path of least resistance in an effort to get to our self-determined utopia. We believe that nothing but pleasure abounds in that idyllic place, where there is more love and contentment than we can handle at one time, and there's no such thing as overindulgence. However, reality is poised to keep us grounded if we allow it to shine its light on flawed thoughts. Feeling loved was my Shangri-La. I risked my body and soul for its sake and walked away unsure I'd found my treasure. I questioned if what I had was real. In spite of everything, I wasn't angry with love or the commitment I made to embrace its power and greatness. Because there are no guarantees, real love is so special. I believed that when love is shared, it's the most beautiful thing in the world. When it replicates and attaches itself to others, pieces of joy are cast throughout generations. I was good at giving love to others; I forgot to give it to myself first.

My eyes were opening as the shades of denial were overtaken by the light of acceptance. I could no longer hide behind the veil of disbelief and complacency. It could no longer be my crutch. I had to pay attention to my needs and stop waiting for someone else to make me feel whole. That would be the only way if I had any hope of changing my brokenness status. I had always been the answer to my own problems. Once I acknowledged that fact, everything changed for me in the blink of an eye. I felt like a different person, inside and out. I wanted to run to the mirror to see if the reflection showed a vision of my former self. I'd been so disfigured by abuse and shame that I forgot what I looked like. My body and my soul ached for revival. I could feel relief spreading inside.

Existing in the shadows inhibits growth. I'd existed in the shadows of a man who didn't deserve me as a wife, mother, woman, or friend. Initially, I thought I could change Carter. As we grew closer together, I believed some of me would merge with the thin places in his character that needed attention. It was humbling to admit my misgivings. I came to him inflated with hope. Over time, the air was kicked, slapped, and punched out of me until I resembled a deflated balloon. I couldn't fix the external nicks that caused a slow leak in my heart. He cheated and abused me. I said nothing and did nothing. I hated to admit that I was the biggest problem I had. The irrational fear that I wasn't good enough to be loved traumatized me. It held me hostage as much as the mental bars that kept me terrified of walking out of doors that were never locked. Healing myself would eliminate so many of the thoughts and fears that enslaved me. I was tired of the false smiles and painted lies masquerading as truth. I needed to restore my inner peace. It was long overdue.

I couldn't exorcise the things I couldn't leave behind. Eventually, that list would include Carter. His assault on Eva changed me in more ways than I immediately understood. I had to face some truths that had been hindered by my aversion to our marital problems. I'd spent the bulk of my marriage hiding from things too unpleasant to face, but I couldn't hide from the truth forever. Eventually, it found me. I gave my life away for too many years, now it was time to take it back. I couldn't get back the time I lost on something that wasn't meant to work. It was time to wave the white flag. I'd lost myself for several years and was overjoyed to find me again. My happiness had been postponed long enough. Moment by moment, I was finding my center and learning that I could stand on my own. I couldn't beat myself up about the choices I'd made that still affected me. I'd been through enough beatings already. It was time to forgive myself.

Eva's and my mother's words echoed through my head about my importance to my children. It was my time to shine as a mother. At first, their job was to protect me. It was a selfish concept that ended up being more of a blessing than I deserved. They continuously outperformed my expectations, even after their tenure as protectors ended. Now it was my job to nurture them into decent humans filled with love, honesty, and respect. I didn't want to breathe our dysfunction into our children. It would be abusive. I didn't know what was lurking on the branches of a disfigured family tree I needed to prune. If I didn't show them what it looked like to live a life full of decency and love, maybe I'd find the faces of my children. Without my example, their hearts were destined to be brittle and unkind. I was unwilling to accept that risk. One cardiac episode in the family was enough. I had to heal my heartbreak and show that power to my children. If I didn't make some drastic changes to my life, the pain and disappointment of an unhealthy relationship would outlast me and become a legacy of defeat for my children. They deserved better.

Thankfully, my world was falling apart. I was dropping layers of pretend like wilted flower petals. It was time to decide what I wanted my life to look like and who I wanted to be in it. A friend once shared folklore that had been passed down through their family. Each person stands in front of a mirror, closes their eyes, and thinks of someone in their life. If there's a smile on their face when their eyes reopen, that person should remain in their life. If not, they should be removed. The moral suggests that we should only be surrounded by those who add something meaningful to our lives. I closed my eyes and blinked through a list of people that included friends, family, and Eva. Each time I blinked and opened my eyes, there was a smile on my face. None was there when I thought about Carter or myself. Something had to change.

Chapter Forty-Nine

Falling

I was changing, not out of fear, but because of strength I'd buried under many layers of make-up, clothes, shoes, houses, cars, hurt, disease, bruises, and lies. It was time to let go and free-fall from the perch I'd sat on for many years. It would be painful as the jagged rocks of reality exposed my sensitivity to change. I didn't know what awaited me on the last few rungs of my downward descent, but I'd be glad when I reached the bottom. I wanted absolutely no unfinished emotional baggage to unpack.

For a long time, I dreaded the inevitable. I couldn't perpetuate the lifestyle I'd settled for long past the emotional end of our marriage. I had no choice now. Carter's actions had taken that away from me. I was on my own. I couldn't figure out who I was madder at, him or myself. I'd be in the valley soon and couldn't fall any further down. The closer I got to the bottom, the more like myself I felt, but different. The landing was softer than I'd anticipated. Hitting the bottom was painfully peaceful. It knocked the wind out of me momentarily and I was cracked in several places, but not totally broken. I knew I'd be able to recover from the fall.

I'd had my mountain moments. I could be content with my valley view. Down in the valley, there was a connection I thought I'd forfeited with my ascension to my status pedestal. I lacked realness and a sense of self. I'd turned my nose up at the world and everyone who loved me and almost drowned from the raindrops. I'd been too involved in a game of make-believe that never allowed me to recognize anything real. A cool mist washed over me and cleansed the remaining mask that didn't get wiped off as I brushed up against fragments of my illusion. I looked around and began to see what I couldn't from my perch above everything and everybody. The things that looked so small and insignificant from my prior vantage point became larger than life. I could see details that I previously overlooked. I began to appreciate the beauty in my new location more than I thought was possible.

The waters of depth I thought dried up years earlier, instinctively found their way to hidden streams that flowed into the rivers of my upbringing, values, and self-esteem. I could feel myself being saturated with hope. The forbidden fruit of complacency hung from the branches within my immediate reach. I ignored it. I was inspired to keep moving forward and assume an active role in my life. I couldn't be the poor soul who got out of a physical prison only to be locked up mentally. Like Andy from Shawshank, I wanted my life back. I wanted to spread my wings again. Unlike nature's limitations, my clipped wings could be regenerated. I would be able to fly again, even with just one wing. As long as I was able to flap, I had hope. I'd been thrown out of my nest and encountered so many bumps and bruises along the way. I needed the ice of reality to soothe those places and help with the swelling. I felt my head shrinking and my ego returning to normal. I breathed in the fresh air of a new life and exhaled the aroma of peace.

I allowed the residue from years of unrealistic longings to finally exit my soul. It had stymied me for too long and blocked the natural healing process. It was time to collect the broken pieces of my past into baskets of hope and prepare for restoration. I didn't want to look back, only forward. There was no point of lingering where the present would never exist, where courage was abated, and I was destined to wither away into a pile of dust. Maybe it wouldn't happen as fast as Lot's wife, but I'd experience the same ritualistic effect.

To move forward, the lies I believed about myself had to change. The power of my inner voice had far-reaching effects on my soul's transformation. I had to re-wire my thinking so that past emotional triggers no longer controlled me. I'd already learned that even if things once considered vital were taken away, I could survive. I was so fearful of being rejected that I was constantly reaching for something insignificant to wrap my love around. I never realized all I had to do was reach for myself. I was willing to stay in the valley for as long as it took the seeds of my new life to germinate. Once my roots were established, I could stand on my own and grow upward, like saplings stretching toward the heavens.

Chapter Fifty

Verdict

"WRPE is live in front of the courthouse with this update. It's been nearly a year since the arrest of the prominent businessman, Carter Mann. As you recall, the defendant is being tried for brutally assaulting a pregnant woman who was not his wife. Paternity tests confirmed that the child she was carrying was, in fact, the daughter of Mr. Mann. The defense will rest its case today before final arguments. The jury is expected to begin deliberations by midday."

It took less than three hours for the intersection of testimony and jury deliberation to return a guilty verdict that surprised no one. Carter shook his head in disbelief but remained silent. The confluence of emotions that gripped me, caught me off guard. I was surprised when the validation of my pain caused me to weep openly. To the world, it appeared my tears were those of sadness. I knew my tears were those of release from a history of ugly secrets being pushed from the shadows and publicly recorded as inhumane. I was being comforted by hugs of peace that had been searching for me. The places within, that held tension and bruises from angry hands, released their grip.

Carter's mother put her arm around my shoulder and said, "It's ok Grace. Everything is gonna be fine."

She was exactly right. I was gonna be just fine. I would no longer have to live in hiding. I was free. Carter looked back at me with an expression that said, "This is all your fault." My eyes moved from the beast to the beauties celebrating the jury's decision. Eva and her mother had gotten justice. So had I. It was hard not to smile.

"We interrupt this broadcast for an update on the Carter Mann assault trial. Guilty. That was the verdict from the jury for prominent businessman, Carter Mann. Sources inside the courtroom indicated the prosecutor was not surprised by the verdict but noted how quickly the verdict was reached. Victim impact statements will be heard before sentencing recommendations are made. Stay tuned to WRPE for further updates."

After hearing those words several times before getting home, I was mentally exhausted. Our anniversary was only days away. I was relieved that I wouldn't be sitting in court behind my husband as he was being tried for assault against his mistress, the mother of his other child. I'd have to spend it alone, but I would have chosen loneliness over sitting in the middle of such an anomaly.

Instead of looking at my anniversary as a day of dread, in Carter's absence, I decided to make it a day of celebration with my family. Since our anniversary day had been stained by his arrest, I wanted to change its complexion and replace those memories with fresh ones created by the joy on the face of our children. Maybe the tradition could carry forward as Liberation Day. When the final plans were made, the vacation invitation included my parents and my sister. They deserved something special for having cared for my children when I couldn't.

Chapter Fifty-One

Happy Anniversary

The day before our family trip, Carter's attorney called with a message from him. He wanted me to visit him on our anniversary. I wondered in what alternate universe that would happen. We had nothing to celebrate. He was still trying to control me from behind bars, and I was still laughing when I hung up the phone. After the laughter subsided, I was forced to deal with what was coming the next day. Even though I tried to replace its significance with something else, the ring on my finger served as a constant reminder that I was still married. Thoughts of our wedding vows, filled with promises made but not kept, were on my mind as the wine rocked me to sleep.

Disorientation greeted me the next morning as sunlight pierced my squinty eyes. The pillow next to me became my temporary shield from another day. It was too late. I was morning's prisoner. I acknowledged its victory and burrowed deeper into the bedcovers. Eventually, I had to surrender to the new day. My first thoughts were of Carter's request. Before I received the message from him, I was excited about the family vacation I'd planned that would be good for me and our children. I wanted the smell of the ocean and the feel of sand between my toes to comfort me through any awkward reminders of the identity crisis this day represented. After the call, my mind stalled at our wedding ceremony. I was unable to ignore the day's significance.

I had it all worked out in my head, but my heart couldn't hide from the fact that it was our anniversary day. All I kept saying was, "Why this day?" He could've chosen any other random day on the calendar, but he chose to defile the day of our union. I would never escape the memories and disappointment that would be forever associated with what was supposed to be our special day. Instead of being treated by traditional anniversary offerings, I was gifted with a bouquet of regrets along with a heart wounding box of sadness. I was almost surprised, emphasis on almost, by the events of that day. Just like the flowers of spring, I knew the seeds of his infidelity would eventually be in full bloom for all the world to see.

I looked over at the side of the bed where my husband should've been. For the second year, it was empty. No "good morning, baby." No "happy anniversary darling." There was no morning spooning or fingers that magically intertwined, no gentle kisses on my neck, no gentle caressing of my breasts or stroking of my hips and inner thighs from slow-moving hands. There was just me and a bodily yearning for my husband's skillful touch. The explosion of desire startled me but shouldn't have. He was deeply embedded in me. It would take a while for him to leave. I was happy when those feelings ran their course through my mind and body and exited as quickly as they came. I was certain it wouldn't be the last time they would visit. I couldn't deny there were some physical things about him I would miss but not enough for my freedom.

After the events of the past year, I never imagined I would be so emotional about our anniversary day. I had to remember that emotions are fickle and change constantly. From moment to moment, they can be your best friend and your worst enemy. They can propel you to the heights of optimism and the depths of despair. Some of the emotions I felt were about us, as a couple, and others were about how I'd grown up since his arrest. I'd learned how to harness

193

those emotions and not act from a place of desperation. Every year I would remember the day from a different perspective. Since our marriage had finished its course, I would celebrate my transformation from dependent to independent. Maybe this could be remembered as my day of emancipation. I would have plenty of time to figure it out. I put those heavy thoughts away and finished packing my suitcase. I didn't want to miss my flight. It was time for the new tradition to begin.

Chapter Fifty-Two

Final Visit

Each time I visited Carter, the gap between us widened. It became more difficult to endure the visits. Most times, my mind longed to be any place but there. I'd gotten to know another man because of spending time with Eva. Depending on how he looked or the words he said, I couldn't tell if I was talking to Ben or Carter. It was as if an imaginary line vertically separated his face and words were coming out of both sides of his mouth. I wondered if his head would spin if I told him how frequently I talked to Eva. I wanted to tell him but decided it was too cruel. He was suffering enough.

Carter's anger was apparent when I sat down in the visitor's booth and picked up the phone.

"Grace, did you get my message that I wanted to see you on our anniversary day?"

"Yes, I did."

"Then, why weren't you here?"

Internally, I sarcastically mumbled, "Poor Carter. He had to spend our anniversary alone."

"I spent time with our children. I had to explain to them that their father wouldn't be home any time soon."

"You should've been here for me. You can see them anytime. Don't you think you were being selfish?"

"Not as selfish as you think. Between us, there are three children; two of which you support. What do you plan to do about Joy, your other daughter? How much support do you want to offer her mother?"

Carter leaned back in his chair with a disgusted look on his face. Each time I mentioned Eva and his baby, he acted as if they'd magically disappeared. We both knew that, eventually, I would have to interpret that truth for our children.

"Do we really need to talk about that right now? I want to know why you abandoned me. You don't know what I'm going through in here. I need to be home with you and the kids. I wish you could've persuaded Eva to not press charges. We could've spent our anniversary together."

His arrogance was appalling. I couldn't believe he just blamed me for his still being in jail. He remained who he always was. Hoping for a change in his character was pointless. I watched his lips move breath around and formed words I chose not to entertain. They danced around in the air looking for portals to lend credence to the efforts he made to verbally reach me. We were miles apart. I continued to watch his mouth move and substituted his words with my own. They were not pleasant. They were vile and boasted of the superior position I held at that moment. He'd earned every syllable.

I continued to stare directly at him, but my mind was generations away. It was in our past and the future of our children, all three of them. I knew I could only become stronger if I stood up for myself. My eyes met his and stared deep into his soul. I saw shadows, heard screams and cries for help, felt punches and cracking bones, saw twisted bodies, forgotten tears, and tasted a mouth full of metal and gun powder, but there was no true love. It hadn't been there for years, if ever. I burned Carter's image into my mind and closed my eyes for an extended blink. When I opened them, I wasn't smiling. Everything became so clear. I looked at him and said, "Good-bye, Carter. I'll make sure your attorney has your clothes for court."

His facial expression was priceless. He was stunned. His head didn't spin off his body, but his dropped jaw and bulging eyes were sufficient. My words caught him off guard. I didn't give him a chance to say anything before I stood up, dropped the phone, and walked away. The phone swung aimlessly by its cord and waved good-bye to Carter for me. He knew I wouldn't be back. Two days later, I put the house up for sale.

Chapter 53

Baring Souls

"This is WRPE reporting with the latest updates and information. Prominent businessman Carter Mann will be back in court tomorrow for the delivery of the impact statements from the victim and her family. As you recall, the jury returned a guilty verdict in that case. Mr. Mann's victim is expected to make a statement. Stay tuned to WRPE, your information station."

Stories no one ever heard were stamped on my body. A living canvas, highlighted by scars and bruises, became the reference map of my loneliness and isolation. I became a one-of-a-kind portrait of surrender, signed, and numbered by the author of abuse. The aggressive mixtures of words, phrases, and mannerisms led to the same distorted masterpiece that changed so much about me. I wasn't comfortable in sleeveless garments. They could expose scars and other signs of trauma once expressed in vibrant colors of a sunset. From the neck down, the landmarks of angry love were always hidden. My canvas should've been filled with color and life instead of grotesque shadowing that told stories of times I'd suffered out of economic necessity. But he couldn't hurt me any longer. My canvas was ready to be painted with colors of hope and renewal and an acceptance of where I was in my current life. It was time for show-and-tell with my mother. I was about to confirm things she guessed and reveal things she never could imagine.

Pains reminiscent of labor made me pace the floor. Secret burdens, well past full term, were about to be freed from deep within. No longer would the facts be twisted beyond recognition. The truth would hurt, but its legitimacy would no longer be hushed into quietness. Once released, loud cries of self-love would be heard by the world. I knew I was getting closer to the end of this side of my labor. I barely had time to experience much peace. The intermittent pain subsided just long enough for me to catch my breath and brace for what was yet to come.

I understood that what I expelled would make room for the life I was meant to have. The painful memories of my labor would soon be a distant memory. Gone, but not forgotten because of its necessity to the process. The pain would no longer inhabit my being, but the spirit of release would remain. To attain the bundle of joy that awaited me, I couldn't focus on the life I would leave behind. I had to channel all my energy into something I could nurture into strength. Instinctively, I knew it was time to grit my teeth and push forward my truth so no one could use it against me.

When my mother sat down on the sofa, I visually shared my important conversation. I couldn't display pictures of my blackest eyes, most swelled lips, and the deepest bruises that led to lost relationships, unfulfilled promises, and broken dreams. I could only show her what toll Carter's physical abuse had taken on my body. Without saying a word, I stood up, removed my blouse, and exposed some of my darkest secrets. She gasped and covered her mouth with her hands. Her fingers gently touched the places on my body where natural color had been overtaken by healed scars, some deeper than others. I had to look away while her face filled with sadness as her eyes witnessed pieces of my story.

Not far into the reveal, her eyes exploded with tears that showed no judgment, just love. I felt her pain in my soul.

Once I was in her embrace, she rested her chin on my shoulder and pulled me into her bosom. She trembled as she cried anguished tears. I could feel them rolling down my back, spreading love where there once was pain. We both were being healed. After releasing that batch of tears, she pulled me onto her lap, covered my tattered body with my blouse, and rocked me back and forth, just as she did when I was a child. I snuggled in deeper and enjoyed every moment. We talked briefly about a few other things after I put my blouse back on but nothing too heavy. I didn't need to tell her too much more about my troubled marriage. Carter was still my husband and the father of my children. Some secrets and vows were meant to be kept between husband and wife.

Just as I didn't know the effects Carter's actions had on Eva's family, I never imagined what effect my actions had on my own. I never considered my parent's feelings when it came to our marriage. My mother's reactions to viewing some of the darker sides of our marriage exposed my flawed logic. I never stopped being their daughter because I became a married woman. They still prayed for me, cried for me, and worried about me. Being a parent didn't stop at some magic age or with an arbitrary life event. It was their forever identity. My family continued to love me in spite of the protective distance I kept. What a fool I'd been to refuse the anchor they continually offered.

Chapter Fifty-Four

Bloody Shoes

The conversation with my mother was the catalyst that propelled me further into the reclamation process. I looked through the contents of my closet and took a painful walk down memory lane. Over the years, as the abuse became more brutal, the value of the gifts increased. My eyes roamed across the collection amassed from swollen lips, bruised ribs, black eyes, and the devaluing of my worth. The first assault came with a tearful apology and professions of love and regret, supplemented by a designer handbag that I showboated around my family and friends, once my bruising subsided. I remember someone saying, "I know that must have cost a pretty penny." It did, not in dollars and cents, but in self-esteem. I wondered what the gift would've been had I lost vision in my left eye.

I looked at the box that held the pair of Louboutin's. They truly were bloody shoes. I miscarried my first child the night after I wore those shoes. I'd never worn them again. It hurt too much. Not my feet, but my heart. I despised those shoes for what they represented. I didn't know why I held on to them for so long. Maybe I liked the pain that rippled through my being that signaled I still had the capacity to feel something. Perhaps the aroma of the shoes connected me to the child I lost. They became the outward expression of a secret no one knew, and I refused to share. I closed my eyes and thought about what could've been. I often daydreamed about echoes of laughter, snapshots of dimpled cheeks, turned-up corners of a mouth, and eyes that showed nothing but love for me. But those illusions only existed in my mind. It was for the sheer pleasure of those brief moments that I kept the shoes with the many other secrets I stowed away as my abuse mementos.

I got out those same shoes and couldn't control the tears that flowed like a sprinkler onto the surface of the dust bag. I rubbed my hand over the tears while preparing my heart to revisit painful reminders of loss. My hands trembled as they made their first contact with the supple leather of the shoemaker's masterpiece. I was sure it took a master craftsman a lot of time and effort to perfect the ultimate finished product. It had taken my husband a considerable amount of time and effort to yield the finished product I became. I, too, had been hidden in a box for years. I turned the shoe over and gazed at how cheerfully the bright red color jumped at me. The smell of high-quality leather was appealing to my senses. I filled my lungs to capacity, not realizing that haunted memories would infiltrate this reunion. I sucked in my breath as my heart quickened in response to the phantom memories of a heartbreaking loss. I dropped the shoes to the floor, covered my mouth, and raced to the bathroom when the taste and smell of old blood in my mouth produced an aroma of defeat. I had to vomit. I barely made it to the sink.

Sweating profusely, I stood over the vent, then slowly slid down the wall. That same tile floor greeted me again, the same as it did that day. The tile wasn't judgmental, selective, or irrational. It greeted all with the same hardness and its cold touch. It knew me well. Over the years, it had accepted deposits of everything my battered body left behind. I had fallen in the bathtub was the story. His foot had fallen into my abdomen was the truth. I often wondered what the room would've looked like were it ever sprayed with luminol. The splashes of color exhibited on the tiles would have outlined the overlapping scenes of pain that only the two of us had witnessed. Like a true friend, the tile never shared my secrets. It always caught me and allowed me to lean on it as long as I needed. Once again, it didn't let me fall.

I made my way back into the bedroom and looked at the shoes again. They would remain connected to too much pain unless I changed their voice. Until then, they could only speak of pain and defeat. I needed them to speak of triumph and freedom. I picked up the shoes and slowly put in one foot, then the other. They still knew me and welcomed me back into their world. I became overwhelmed by strength and hope. Then, I stood up.

I was afraid to move once I had the shoes on. I feared the weight of my life and the heaviness connected to the shoes would cause me to topple over. But I had to try to move forward. I took the first step, dropped to my knees, and cried. I couldn't give up. I was ready to shed the things that held me in bondage. Once I stood up again, I was a giant. I regained my balance, centered myself, and began to walk around the room, dripping tears that were stepped on by the cheerful red soles of my shoes. With each step I took, sorrow was ground into obscurity by my strength. I felt the curvature in my slumped over spirit becoming erect. I was ready to be free.

I laid in bed thinking about what would happen when I went back inside that courtroom. I'd endured unimaginable situations during our marriage that had been put on trial along with my husband. In my darkest times, it seemed my world, and sometimes the end of my life, was near, but hope always found a way to renew itself in me. I believed that if the new day was one iota better than the previous one, I had a reason to fight. Each new breath confirmed I was one day closer to being whole again.

The person I was, before my life with Carter, moved inside my soul. At one time, I thought I'd lost her, but there she was, a little neglected, but still alive and ready to be refreshed. When I looked in the mirror, I saw her flickering light trying to catch fire in my spirit. She was different from the one who stared back at me a year ago. Her transformation had been steady and impactful. I couldn't help but acknowledge the debt I owed Eva. From the first day I met her, and she embraced me in my sorrow, my life changed. For so many reasons, I would demonstrate my appreciation for her in court.

Chapter Fifty-Five

Victim Impact Statement

Throughout the trial, I'd been a dutiful wife, but it was time to do something for myself. I was no longer afraid to let everyone see how I felt. I was tired of being an imposter. It was time that I took a seat on the justice train. There was a vacant seat behind Eva.

One of Carter's attorney's smiled as I walked into the courtroom, flawless as ever, wearing my bloody shoes. She didn't realize the significance of my footwear. Her smile quickly faded when I walked to the other side of the courtroom. With cameras flashing and people reacting, my courage grew. When I reached Eva, we embraced and I whispered in her ear, "Thank you" before taking a seat in the gallery behind her. His mother would have to sit by herself. Everyone heard me, even though they didn't see my lips move.

It had taken a lot of strength to not sit behind my husband that day. My decision was one I needed in order to move forward. Before I sat down, I quickly looked over toward Carter's attorney. I saw her whisper in his ear before he turned around and stared at me. Eyes filled with a look of disapproval launched glances filled with threats in my direction. I heard every word with my eyes. Clearly, he was agitated, but I didn't care. He couldn't hurt me anymore. For someone who didn't want to be painted in a negative light, he showed his true self to everyone sitting in the room. He was fortunate the judge hadn't entered the courtroom while his attorney struggled to restrain him. His mother got up from her seat, had a brief conversation with her son, and sat back down. His agitation waned. I expected to see the same disapproving glare from Carter's mother. To my surprise, her face stayed neutral and never looked in my direction. I feared I would face her wrath once we finally spoke.

As I sat in the gallery behind Eva and her mother, I wondered if I'd been emotionally compromised by my relationship with her. Could my regard for her and Joy caused me to betray my husband? That would be something I would have to figure out in seasons to come. But that day, I was where I needed to be, supporting the person who fought for me and the child I lost when I didn't have the strength or the courage to fight for myself. I owed her the public show of support more than anyone would ever understand.

Two hours after court began, I sat in silence in the courtroom. I remained behind, hoping to escape the scrutiny of those with questions I didn't want to answer. As anticipated, Carter's mother came over and sat beside me. I prepared for harsh words and her disapproval of my alliance with Eva.

After she embraced me, she said, "Grace, I'm so proud of you for finally standing up for yourself. Carter is so much his father's son."

I wasn't prepared for her show of admiration. The look on my face prompted her to ask, "What's the matter, Grace, you don't believe me?"

"Well, I'm surprised. I thought you'd be mad at me for abandoning your son."

"No, I understand why you did it. If I was mad about anything, it was about your staying with him so long, especially after how he's treated you."

I was really shocked. "I don't mean any harm, but I thought you didn't like me."

"Well, to be honest with you, I didn't at first."

"Wow. I didn't expect that."

"Now, let me explain. My feelings about you were not for the reason you imagine. Initially, I was afraid for you and then became afraid of you."

"Why?"

"I was afraid for you because I knew who my son was. Just like his father, he was hooked on control. I sensed the beautiful innocence in you. I knew my son would eventually suck it out of you with his cruelty."

My eyes welled up with tears. I heard a truth I'd tried to understand for years. His infidelity and cruelty had nothing to do with me. I was blameless. I couldn't fix him. He was broken at a level I couldn't reach.

"Grace, years ago, when we had our private lunch, you broke my heart. You made me see myself and the ugliness I'd accepted that masqueraded as love. I saw myself in your devotion and love for my son. I'd been the same way with his father. While I'd hoped your life would've been better than mine, I feared it wouldn't. I wanted to tell you to leave him, but I knew it wouldn't have done any good. I saw the love you had for my son in your eyes."

She was right. I truly loved Carter. "I really wanted our marriage to work. But sometimes he let his anger get out of control. I was scared of him."

"I always thought that some of my nurturing would be enough to quell the cruelty beast that lurks beneath the surface in all of us. But I saw glimpses of the demon in Carter as he got older. You made me see that I hadn't saved him. I'd failed. I'd handed you a broken man. That's who his father and I taught him to be. Your love didn't have a chance."

I looked at my hand and started fidgeting with my wedding ring. Tears began to roll down my face, not for regret but release.

His mother took my hand and said, "Don't ever think it wasn't okay to love him. That's who you are. Never let anyone tell you that loving someone is ever wrong. It's the greatest gift we can ever give someone. If you lose your capacity to love, you've lost everything."

Through the flow of tears, I said, "I tried. I really tried."

"I know, honey. I know. I love you for trying." She allowed me to dry my tears before she said, "Grace, I don't think you really understand what you did for us today."

"Us?"

"Yes, your actions spoke for me as much as they did for Eva. You spoke for our bloodline today. You said that we'd had enough. I saw what happens to our children when we don't speak up. It lays the groundwork for another generation of brokenness. We, including you and Eva, have to love our next generation into improvement. Today was a good start. I love my son, but I don't condone what he did. I even take some blame. But, he has to be held accountable for his actions. Maybe prison will turn out to be the best thing for him."

The reality of Carter's situation hit me. He was going to prison. Our children would spend years without their father. I would miss him too, but that ugly part of my life was finally over.

I leaned into her as Carter's mother put her arm around my shoulder. We sat quietly before she said, "Grace, I have a feeling you're gonna be just fine. After today, no one can ever question your strength. Now it's time to focus your thoughts and energy on those two beautiful children. Love them deeply and protect them fiercely. Use our lessons to teach them there is goodness in all of us, no matter who we come from, and we, as individuals, make the choice about who we choose to be. Now, I think I've said enough for one day. It's time for you to go live your life with no guilt or shame. I'll be there for my son. It's the least I can do."

After Carter's mother hugged me, she stood up, moved into the aisle, and said, "And Grace,"

"Yes, ma'am."

"Don't forget to look sad and a bit lost for a while. That worked for me."

I smiled and said, "I'm sure I can do that."

Carter's mother winked at me and strolled toward the exit. When she got to the end of the gallery, she turned around and said, "Just between us women, the day my husband took his last breath was one of the best days of my life. If you're wise, you may want to consider this one of your best days, as well."

She blew me a kiss and disappeared into the hallway. Something about her tone let me know that the truth was still being uncovered in that courtroom. In a moment of introspection, I sat in silence absorbing all that transpired that day. The aura of peace that surrounded me helped release a thousand pounds of regret. My soul celebrated. When I stood up, I looked down at my shoes. Tears rushed toward them in celebration. I knew I would never wear those shoes again; my baby had gotten its day in court. Eva gave us a voice. It was time to emerge from hiding. I whispered, "Olly, Olly oxen free" to myself before I pushed open the courtroom door and walked away from a life that no longer suited me. I didn't return to court after that day. I learned of his sentence with the masses. There was no reason to return after the last statement I made. My prayers were answered in ways I never imagined. The beginning of his sentence meant the end of mine.

"This is WRPE news reporting with an update on the Carter Mann trial. In a moment that stunned most people in the courtroom, the wife of Carter Mann broke ranks and sat with the victim of her husband's attack as victim impact statements were being heard. Sources confirm a brief conversation was held between Mrs. Mann and the victim before court got underway. Mr. Mann and his defense team were surprised by that unusual sight. Whether or not this move will impact sentencing is yet to be seen. We will keep you informed with further news and updates."

Chapter Fifty-Six

Letting Go

After two weeks on the market, my dream house on the hill, behind the black iron gates, had been sold. That house was no longer the place I needed to be. My children and I deserved a fresh start in a place that would usher in a life we couldn't have experienced had we remained trapped behind those gates. A smaller house near my parents made the transition easier for us and gave me a chance at a completely new life. In my new home, I wanted to experience the parts of life that happen in quiet spaces when there is no grandeur, but real living occurs.

Standing on the porch, before my final walkthrough, caused mixed reactions. A new family would walk through those doors filled with hopes and dreams similar to those I brought with me. I remembered the kiss, the squeals of excitement, and the smiles as Carter swung open the front door, gathered me in his arms and carried me into our new home. I also remembered how everything changed that cool October evening with one knock, two officers, and a desperate request three days later. After witnessing Carter's hands cuffed behind his back, I no longer wanted to stand under the lights on that front porch. It reminded me of how Carter brought all of his mess home, left it on our doorstep, and expected me to clean it up. Our lives began a downward spiral that didn't stop until a verdict was rendered. It marked the beginning of my freedom.

A stream of light filtered through the window blinds and marked its territory on the hardwood floors. It revealed tiny particles of dust caught up in a stream of moving air. Shadow patterns danced on the floors as I moved further into the place I once called home. So many years of my life had been spent within the confines of these walls. It wasn't all bad. When Carter carried me into the new house, I entered full of smiles and expectations of a happy life. Although there were happy times, there just wasn't enough of them to keep the bad times from making a lasting impression on me.

Up in my castle on top of the hill, I felt trapped. I didn't see a way out without ruining everything I'd worked so hard for. As much as I hated the inside, it frightened me when I thought about what life would be like beyond the window. The moat that surrounded me wasn't full of alligators or snakes, it was full of prior sins I was afraid would eat me alive. That constant fear kept me too weak to run and always regretful when I stayed. But all that was changing. I was no longer trapped. The doorway to freedom had cracked open, and I was running toward the exit.

Memories encircled me as I slowly wandered through the empty space. Pieces of my soul were still floating around inside, even though I hadn't lived there for months. Everywhere I turned, there were reminders of what I sacrificed for my version of a life that never materialized. Many days, I woke up with hope but laid down with heartache when brutality resulted from accusations of a wandering eye, wearing the wrong dress, inappropriate exposure of my body, words not spoken quickly enough or a bedroom performance not good enough. All became scapegoats for his breach of kindness. My mind resurrected the past as echoes from screams of fear rang in my ears. I rubbed the place where the coarseness of his palm met the skin against my face. I felt the walls groan from the sudden weight of my body before its identity transformed into a temporary sliding board. I heard the thud after my body kissed the floor. With wildness in his voice and bewilderment in his eyes, he shouted my list of indiscretions while he dragged, kicked, and propelled me across the room. Cries for mercy and offers of obedience, in exchange for relief, bounced around the room. I witnessed the silence rescue me from his anger, my body collapse in relief, and my prayers being answered too late. I wanted to cover my ears and run out of the house but knew I needed to let those ghosts rattle at me one last time. After I exited the premises, they'd have to find another host.

Many days, I was lonely in a space where, by definition, there should be peace and love. Inside a house filled with silence, I wished love would rain on me as heavily as the loneliness. I needed someone to talk to who wouldn't judge me and would never break my trust. I wanted to talk about every hurt that had been thrust upon me and every unrepentant prayer I whispered for an illness to ravage Carter's body. Since therapy was out of the question, I eventually started talking to myself. Getting out the angry words I couldn't share with him preserved my sanity. I kept it just between me and the walls. It was the only outlet I trusted. If some of the walls could laugh, they'd have a comedic treasure trove of material based on my unattainable desires. Other walls would cry for me. They witnessed my darkest terror-filled moments, tasted my blood, and absorbed the sound of my anguished tears.

The sense of relief I felt after the verdict didn't remain long. With it, I also experienced sadness. I told my heart to detach and stop feeling anything for Carter, but it wouldn't listen. Love was meant to be shared, not used as a weapon of control. Before he was prosecuted, I believed he just needed a little time to find his way back to me. I was always ready to smother him with a hoarder's load of love. I kept watering the artificial flowers of his love, waiting for them to grow. They never did. Even with everything that happened during our marriage, I always held a piece of my heart in protective custody. I saved it for Carter; a space where love was stored that I would have expanded to invite him back in. I was always ready to forgive all if he could just love me. For years I was willing; he wasn't able. At this point, I was no longer willing. I thought about how my life could've been, had there been a true commitment from my husband to the matrimonial vows. For a long time, I wanted him back. Not anymore. It was time to let him go. It was time to move on. His prison sentence made sure I could completely walk away.

My life's novel contained many unread pages of a story longing to be heard. But Carter wasn't interested in the pristine pages that never connected with human hands. Groups of letters blackened the pages of a manuscript whose indented trenches produced untouched areas of my essence. The beautifully written novel never got the attention of the one audience I longed to capture. For the sake of our children, I wanted us to be friends. During my last visit to the jail, he demonstrated how complicated that would be. Friends supported each other. I didn't think we could be friends. Maybe my feelings would change after I forgave him. Eva was right when she said I would know when I was ready to forgive Carter. I still wasn't there yet. It would probably take a long time, a sentiment Eva's mother and I shared. I had at least five years to work on it.

I stood in the spot where my sofa used to be and thought about the dream I had during the storm. I marveled at how its coded message finally made sense. I would never forget the impact of that subconscious encounter. It reminded me of the challenge that awaited me and that I had all I needed to survive. As I took a final tour of my bedroom, I was drawn to the window. From there, I saw the place by the fence where the uprooted tree once rested. I'd planted a new tree in the same location. Before anchoring it in the ground, I wrote down all the bad things about my marriage

I wanted to leave behind, put them in a box, and placed it underneath the roots. Deep in the earth, I'd stowed away a box full of sorrow that wouldn't be freed within my lifetime. That day was the perfect time and place to leave it all behind. While I was writing things to put in the box, I wrote a short note to my eight-year-old self:

Dear Grace,

Fix the doll's leg.

A conflux of emotions overtook me when I exited the house for the last time. The final chapter in my book of fantasy had been read. It didn't end the way I envisioned, but I was overjoyed by the alternate ending. Something totally unexpected had been lifted from tattered pages and used to start a new manuscript. I couldn't wait for the sequel. One of my greatest strengths was my ability to compartmentalize my true feelings in order to guard my heart. I didn't need that skill anymore. My heart was open again. The things I was leaving behind couldn't hurt me anymore. They had fueled me to greater things and became milestones of my transformation. Each time I took something away, I expected my life to topple, but to my surprise, I remained standing, even without the pieces I sacrificed. My new path had already led me to places where I could be myself. I was determined to find the life I'd always dreamed about, even though it would be without my husband. I couldn't have gotten to that place in life and understood the capacity of the human spirit without the lessons demonstrated by one genuine embrace from a stranger.

Once I got in my car and started my descent down the hill, I didn't look back. Through the rear-view mirror, I saw my past, as well as my former home, get smaller and smaller, until they no longer could be connected to the woman I was to become. When I got to the bottom of the hill, I stopped and put the car in park. I sat there quietly thinking about how much more my life was about to change. I adjusted the rear-view mirror, looked into it, and closed my eyes. When I opened them again, I was smiling.

The End

Epilogue

I'd been following the Carter Mann trial for about a year. Watching it unfold from the arrest to the verdict had been one of the highlights of my lonely existence. Part of me sympathized with the accused because I'd stood on both sides of the fence. There were times when I'd lost control when it came to a woman. Admittedly, it hadn't been my finest moment. But nothing compared to the time when a woman had lost control with me, and I ended up suffering consequences that will impact me for the rest of my life. I would have gladly traded places with him. He got his day in court where a verdict was rendered by a jury, not by some crazed woman hell-bent on revenge who took the law into her own hands.

Guilty was the verdict for Carter Mann, who was accused of getting his girlfriend pregnant and assaulting her into premature childbirth. The press conference was just a formality and a bragging opportunity for the prosecutor. Faces of the crowd surrounded the prosecutor as she stood on the steps of the courthouse. The mixture of skin tones and garments reminded me of a human kaleidoscope that constantly changed shapes and colors. The myriad of microphones being shoved in her face looked like black and silver ice cream cones. The overlapping voices that shouted quickfire questions she didn't have time to answer reminded me of an auction. When the camera panned the crowd, the image of a ghost entered the frame. My brain couldn't focus on anything but that vision.

I got up from my chair to take a closer look. It couldn't be. There stood the woman from my past that I'd spent years trying to forget. I'd recognize her anywhere. She was a little older but probably still just as evil. I sure hope Carter Mann wasn't mixed up with her or her daughter. What she did to me with that knife ruined my life. After fifteen years, the trauma she caused still felt fresh. I should have spoken up about what happened that day, but I wasn't sure it would have made much of a difference. What she did to me couldn't change, and I probably would've ended up in jail. I still have so many questions that only that mother and daughter can answer. Maybe it was time to find them.

Acknowledgements

I could not have done any of this without my faith in God, because without it, none of this would have been possible. He continues to give me words that I hope will change someone's life. I also want to thank my family and friends. During the times when I questioned my own abilities, you guys have supported me throughout this process, without hesitation. There were many times when your jokes, prayers, phone calls, and messages of encouragement have propelled me forward.

In addition to my family and friends were those who validated the direction of my work without knowing it. There was the spiritual leader whose talking points during the "Women's Night Out" program expressed some of the thoughts and sentiments already in my manuscript. He gave us a "mission" as he challenged us women not to defer our greatness. I am so glad I was part of that audience.

There was the historical fiction writer, JV, whose infectious passion about her writing journey inspired me to keep moving forward. She offered words of encouragement, resources, and kindness. I will never forget how open and welcoming she made me feel. I want to do the same thing for someone else.

I always listen to and observe the world around me. Since I never meet a stranger, I am often amazed by stories I hear, and sometimes versions of them find their way into my manuscript. After he read my first book, R.R., from St. Louis, shared a family story with me at a softball field in Knoxville. My interpretation of his words can be found in the chapter entitled "Changing Directions" and in another chapter that I won't disclose. I don't want to ruin it for him!

I want to salute the friends who sacrificed their time to help me with this project. I hope you will know who you are from the descriptions. Thank you all from the bottom of my heart. The list includes the following people: Dione the Rapper, The Dorm Runner, Call Me "Kirk", Church Lady "C", NuGene's Brother and The Circus Runaway.

Sometimes, the people who work behind the scenes often get overlooked, but there is no way I can overlook the work of my editing team, Campbell and Clark. These ladies were truly amazing to work with. They pushed me with their honesty and their desire for me to have the best story possible. Ladies, I salute you. I'm already thinking about book three, so I guess you're stuck with me!

For my dad, mother, and brother, who are watching from heaven, you guys continue to inspire me. Dad, your initials are the basis for my pen name. You will be a part of everything I write. Your positive influence on my life continues through my stories. I hope that I continue to make you proud!